Praise for

CITIZEN LOUIS-

CW00400639

"Told in the naïve and endearing voice of an innocent child whose life is determined by bewildering forces and facts he struggles to understand. The story is gripping . . . . The boy is so charming, and his situation so terrible, the reader cannot give up hoping for small mercies."

--- Professor Michael R. Brent,
Washington University.

This novel explores "darkness, loneliness, and cruelty, but also love, strength, and childhood innocence ... Ultimately, woven through the politics of revolution and power, the reader is subtly guided to perhaps the most fundamental question of all: Is a life defined by external circumstances or internal fortitude?"

--- Allen Newcomb

Also by Lizzi Wolf

Athena's Shield:
A novel of the Spartacus Slave Revolt
(2022)

The Versailles of Sadness:
A Novel
(2022)

Citizen Louis-Charles

A novel based on the brief life of

Louis XVII

Lizzi Wolf

MEDUSA BOOKS
2022

A note to readers

Citizen Louis-Charles is the second edition of my novel originally titled *The Orphan King*. Same novel – different title.

1

The Darkness
1794

I am King Louis XVII, supreme monarch of France, but my realm of influence is no bigger than a dank, rat-infested storage closet in the tower of a Medieval castle.

I used to think a King is someone who goes out hunting each morning and returns with dozens of boars, stag, partridge, and hare, to be roasted on a spit and served for supper. I used to worry that I wouldn't be a good King, because I don't like to kill things.

Now I know a King is someone whose family is dragged out of bed in the middle of the night and forced to live in a strange place, surrounded by blood-thirsty mobs and teaming with poison-wielding assassins.

When I was born, no one expected me to become King. My brother, Louis-Joseph, as the first-born son, was the Dauphin, a title given to the heir because our family crest is a dolphin. But Joseph was sickly and died when he was seven. With my brother's death, I became the Dauphin.

My family was still mourning our loss when, three months later, our life unraveled. I was only four. But I noticed things. I remember things. Now that I'm nine, I remember more clearly than ever.

Our troubles began in the Autumn of 1789.

4 ½ years earlier . . .

"Wake up, Dauphin!"

Madam Campan was shaking my shoulder.

The windows were dark.

"It's not morning yet."

"*Shhh*. Get out of bed."

"Why?"

"We're going to the Queen's bedchamber."

My sister Marie was already up. Madam Campan hurried us along the hallway. At the top of the stairs, I pulled back, afraid I would tumble to the marble floor and crack my head open.

"Go," Madam Campan said.

"Hurry up, *bouffon*," Marie said from the bottom of the stairs.

Marie was ten and bossy.

Madam Campan blew out the candle and set it on the floor. She scooped me up and hurried down, then set me on my feet and grabbed my hand to drag me along another dark hallway. Only then did I notice the sounds of people in the garden, whooping and hollering, like Maman's friends when she sets off fireworks.

"Who are they?" Marie asked.

"*Shhh*," Madam Campan hissed.

"What are they celebrating?" I asked.

I heard glass breaking. Wood cracking. The shouting built and crashed, built and crashed, like waves on the shore of Normandy.

"They've broken into the Chateau." Marie sounded afraid.

Whoever they were, these were not Maman's friends.

"Hurry!"

Two Swiss Guards stood at the double doors to Maman's bedchamber.

"I have the Princess and the Dauphin," Madam Campan whispered.

The guards opened the doors and we rushed in. Maman was standing by the bed in her chemise.

"Maman!" I ran into her arms.

"My little sweetheart," she cooed, hugging me and kissing the top of my head.

She pulled aside her nightstand and tapped the flowered wallpaper with her toes. It cracked and caved inward. She crouched down to crawl through the miniature doorway. z

"Come," she whispered.

I stood there, my mouth gaping. I had heard of secret passageways in fairy tales. But I never knew we had one of our own. She didn't even have to say, "Open sesame!"

"Go," Marie hissed, shoving me into the hollow darkness.

I tripped on the first step, falling to my hands and knees. The stone was cold and rough. Dank air, like in a mausoleum, wafted up from the depths of a bottomless stairwell.

Maman disappeared up the steep winding stairs. I crawled to the next step on my palms and toes, like a monkey.

"Wait for me!" I cried.

"Just go," Marie whispered harshly. I heard shouting from the other side of the bedchamber door. Marie grabbed me around the waist, forcing me upward. "Keep climbing."

I climbed into the darkness, my sleeping shirt hanging loose from my belly. A deathlike chill rose up from below.

Maman crouched at the top of the stairs. "It's locked from the other side," she said. "*Damn* Louis and his locks and keys."

It was the first time I had ever heard Maman *damn* Papa. That's when I knew something truly terrible was happening to us.

Madam Campan pushed past Marie and me to help Maman.

"What's the magic word?" I asked.

"There is no magic word, *imbécile*," Marie whispered behind me.

"Louis?" Maman called out, as she and Madam Campan kicked the door. "Marie, come help us."

Marie shoved me aside, making me fall to the next lower step.

"One . . . two . . . Three!" Maman chanted.

With three of them kicking, the door opened, and they tumbled in. I scrambled up the last few steps to find myself in Papa's bedchamber. The shouting of the intruders, bursting into Maman's room, rose up from the stairwell.

"Where is the Queen?" they yelled.

"We want the Queen!"

"Give us the Baker's Wife!"

We searched Papa's room to see if he was hiding, whispering, "Louis? Louis?"

The shouting stopped. Papa's calm, steady voice, echoed up the stairwell.

"I am your King. What do you want of me?"

"Papa's in *your* room," I said to Maman.

"Hush!" she hissed.

We crowded around the broken secret door to listen.

"We need bread!" a woman shouted. "Give us bread!"

"There is bread in my kitchen," Papa told them, "Please help yourselves."

But they didn't seem to really want bread, because no one asked how to get to the kitchen.

"We are taking you to Paris!" a woman shrieked.

"I will go to Paris with you," he replied. "On one condition."

"No conditions!" a woman roared.

"That you allow my family to come with me."

"Take us to the Queen!" they shouted.

"I will take you to the Queen," Papa said.

"Does he know we're in here?" I whispered.

"He figured it out," Marie said. *"Obviously."*

I knew Maman was scared because she didn't scold Marie for talking to me in a mean voice.

The angry women funneled out of Maman's chamber. Maman set Papa's nightstand upright and placed it in front of the broken secret door.

We huddled in the middle of the room. On the other side of the double doors, the intruders yelled at the bodyguards to move aside.

"They rushed ahead of your father," Maman whispered.

"No entry!" the guards insisted. Their sabers clattered.

"Under the bed," Maman commanded Marie and me.

We crawled under Papa's bed and lay on our tummies, peeking out through the gold fringe.

Maman sat on the edge of the bed. Madam Campan stood next to her.

A guard groaned and was silent. The other guard groaned and was silent.

"They've killed the guards," Marie whispered.

"I know," I said. Even though I didn't know.

The doors bulged inward as dozens of fists and feet and shoulders pushed and pounded and pressed against them.

"Please move aside." Papa's baritone voice resonated through the doors.

I heard his key turning in the lock. Papa loved locks and keys. When he wasn't hunting or eating, I could always find him in his workshop, designing and building intricate locks. He told me he wished he had been born a locksmith instead of a King.

The shouting people rushed in ahead of Papa. From under the bed, I saw dozens of pairs of feet. Their shoes were dusty and dirty. Many were barefoot, their toes crooked and deformed, their nails cracked and caked with mud.

I had never seen such ugly feet. Maman's feet were soft and creamy from soaking in jasmine oil and rose petals. Her toes were pink and perfect, the nails glossy as pearls. The toes filling Papa's bedchamber looked like pebbles along the horse path that led to the stables.

The room grew stuffy with a smell of musk and pine and flesh that reminded me of Papa's stench when he came home from hunting.

"We have the Queen!" They cheered.

"You're ours now, you Austrian Sow!" a woman shrieked at Maman.

"Please," Maman pleaded. "You're hurting me." Later, she told us the woman had yanked her hair, bending her head so far back, it hurt her throat.

Papa's embroidered slippers appeared amidst the forest of legs. He was corpulent and walked slowly. According to Marie, he *wattled*. I was afraid he would sit on the bed and force the mattress down so low, it would squish us to death. Marie looked at me with alarm. She was thinking the same thing.

"Do not lay a hand on my family," Papa said. His voice was calm in a way that said he had no need to out-shout the women who were pressing around him on all sides, screaming into his face, "We want bread! Give us bread!"

"I have agreed to go to Paris," Papa reminded them. "Please allow us to dress."

Their screaming subsided into a group grumble. Papa was doing what they had asked. Now they were disappointed at not having anything else to yell at him about.

"Where is the Princess?" someone shouted. "And the Dauphin?"

Marie and I looked at each other. Maman reached down to signal to us. "Come, children. Show yourselves."

We crawled out from under the bed. The women cheered when they saw us. I was confused by how quickly their anger turned to joy.

Maman stood me between her knees, facing the angry women. Marie stood next to Papa, her arm curved along his wide lower back, his forearm draped across her shoulders.

"*Vive le Dauphin!*" they shouted.

"*Vive la Princesse!*"

Maman had taught me to always smile before the people and to appear *unruffled*. I smiled, even though I was afraid they would tear us to shreds, like Papa's hunting dogs when he threw them a rabbit to reward them for a good hunt.

Marie was smiling, too. Her smile made her look like a miniature version of Maman.

"We have the Baker, the Baker's wife, the Baker's daughter, and the Baker's son," a woman announced.

They ordered us to dress quickly. The women stood watching, as if we were bears in a menagerie. They tittered and whispered, taking note of every piece of clothing as we put it on.

Madam Campan dressed me in my sky-blue satin shoes and brocade waistcoat. Maman stood like a statue of a Greek goddess, gazing up at the ceiling, while Madam Campan fastened each layer of her skirts around her waist.

Marie pulled a frock over her head, her face red with shame.

Papa, fully dressed, sat on the edge of the bed with his face in his hands.

We rode along the road from Versailles to Paris in an oxcart. Thousands of angry women, who had been waiting outside the gates of the chateau, surrounded us, driving us through the pouring rain. Maman was afraid I would catch my death. She wrapped me in more and more layers of blankets, until I couldn't move my arms or legs. Her hand lay on a cask of diamonds, rubies, emeralds, and pearls that sat next to her on the wagon bed. Marie stood up and looked fearlessly at the procession that surrounded us.

We were surrounded by a sea of angry women. Not lilac-scented, fancy-dressed ladies with high, powdered wigs, diamonds on every finger, and ropes of pearls around their necks, like Maman and her friends. These were boney, sickly, bedraggled women. A few sat astride canons pulled by cavalry horses, their legs spread over the muzzles. They shouted mean, threatening words at Maman, called her the Austrian Swine, and sang wicked songs about her.

Swiss guardsmen, who had once pledged their lives to Papa, tromped through the mud, singing along with the angry women.

In front of us, two women carried pikes that held the heads of Papa's bodyguards—the men who had been slaughtered while trying to block the door to his chambers. Globs of blood and fat oozed from their shredded necks onto the faces of the women carrying them.

I didn't know what Maman had done to make these women so angry. But I did know it's never too late to beg forgiveness. I fought to untangle myself from the blankets and stood up, holding onto the side of the wagon. It bounced so violently over the rutted road that I could barely keep my balance.

"Please forgive Maman!" I called out. "She's very sorry!"

But my voice was drowned out by the shouting and jeering and chanting.

The next day, Papa read in the *Paris Journal* that six thousand women had marched to Versailles, determined to bring us to the city, where they could keep an eye on us.

When Maman warned me she was keeping her eye on me, that meant she didn't trust me to behave. That's how I found out the people of France did not trust their King and Queen to behave.

2

The Tower
January 1794

"Get up, King Turd!" Reynard says, kicking my bed. "Your sister is coming to visit."

He tells me the National Convention issued a decree that Marie can visit me. I think this must be a good sign that they have finally realized we are harmless to their Revolution.

"Let's surprise her," Reynard suggests. His suggestions are thinly disguised commands.

He opens the door to a storage room that I've never been curious or brave enough to peek into.

"I don't think Marie likes surprises," I say.

I know by now that Reynard's idea of fun involves cruelty. But I am so excited to be seeing my sister for the first time in nine months that I play along. I don't want him to accuse me of insubordination and punish me by canceling the visit.

"Stand inside the door. When she walks in and I signal you," he says, punching the door, "jump out and say, 'Surprise!'"

The room is windowless and without a hearth. I hesitate, tempted to ask for a candle. But I think better of it. On this day of all days, I do not want to ask too much of Reynard.

He shoves me in, then closes and bolts the door. The room is pitch dark.

How am I supposed to jump out if I'm locked in? I think. But I am his prisoner and must be kept under lock and key at all times. Even within my own locked cell.

I stand so close to the door, my nose touches it. I'm so excited to be seeing Marie, I feel giddy. She turned fifteen in December and the first thing I plan to say is "Happy Birthday!"

But it won't be like it used to be on her birthday, when she would say, "Now I'm *seven* years older than you. You'll *never* catch up with me!" And I would run crying to Maman that Marie said I'll never catch up with her. And Maman would take me in her arms and tell Marie to apologize. And Marie would say, "Why should I apologize for telling the truth?" And Maman would say to her, "Go speak to your father." And I would run after her to find Papa reading a newspaper or a book about the history of the English kings, or fidgeting with locks and keys in his workshop. And Marie would tell him she shouldn't have to apologize for telling the truth. And he would keep reading or fidgeting without looking up, and would make a low, gurgling sound in his throat, because he wasn't listening but knew he was supposed to say something but didn't know what it was. And Marie would look at me and I would be gloating, because neither Papa nor Maman would ever take her side against me, because I was the Dauphin. And Marie would glare at me like I was a spider she wanted to smash beneath her heal.

Now that I'm eight and the King, I will be merciful to my sister on her birthday. I won't be jealous that she is seven years older, and that I'll never catch up to her. Instead, I'll ask if Maman is okay. Reynard and his friends assured me she was guillotined three months ago. They made me cry with descriptions of her head being chopped off and the executioner holding it up by her hair as the crowd cheered, "The Queen is dead!"

But I know she's alive. I can hear the murmur of her heart through the walls and ceiling. A low, comforting hum. Like a lullaby.

4 ½ years earlier. . .

I guess the angry women couldn't find it in their hearts to forgive Maman, because they forced us to live in the Tuileries Palace. Papa told me French Kings lived there for centuries, until Louis XIV, my great-great-great grandfather, moved the royal court to Versailles.

Night and day, mobs of men and women, carrying pikes, pitchforks, axes, scythes, scissors, and butcher knives, surrounded the palace. Papa said many of them were farmers and peasants who had come from the countryside. They chanted terrible things about Maman and shouted that they were going to rip out her intestines and hang her with them.

Not everyone in France hated us, though. Two hundred militiamen arrived from Breton to pledge their loyalty to King Louis XVI.

Maman took me out on the terrace, dressed in the red, white, and blue officer's uniform of the Swiss Guard. The soldiers stood stiffly and saluted me as I picked lilacs from bushes that grew up to the balustrades. I handed a sprig of purple blossoms to each officer.

"You must sniff them," I instructed.

They held the flowers to their noses. "Very sweet, my Dauphin," they said. "What a delightful little boy!" they exclaimed to Maman.

After they marched out, I told Maman, "When I am King, I will hand out lilacs to all of my subjects, so they won't sing terrible songs about me and threaten to murder my Queen."

"That is very wise," she said.

Inside the Tuileries, I was allowed to go wherever I liked. One morning, the smell of pie crust led me to the kitchen, where a dozen cooks were busy chopping and roasting and boiling. When I entered, they paused and looked up from their work.

"Good day, Dauphin," they said.

Except the Pastry Chef, who pulled a tray from the oven and set it on his worktable.

"Are those lemon tarts?" I asked.

"Yes, Citizen Louis," he nodded. "Would you like to try one?"

My name is Louis, like my Papa. But no one outside the Royal Family was supposed to call me anything other than Dauphin.

"I would very much like to have a tart."

The Pastry Chef lifted me onto a stool, set the tart on a plate, and sat next to me.

Servants are not supposed to sit in the presence of royalty. But Maman had warned me, "These are different times, and we must grow accustomed to different ways of doing things. Until your Papa is restored to power."

I tried to pick up the tart, but it burned my fingertips. The Pastry Chef laughed. Not even Marie would have laughed at me for hurting myself.

"Are you a Patriot?" he demanded.

"What's a Patriot?" I replied, sucking my fingers to ease the pain.

"Shame on your mother for not teaching you. A Patriot is a Revolutionary."

"The Revolutionaries hate us."

"We despise the noxious blood of the Bourbon Dynasty. We believe his Majesty is no better than a street sweeper or a slops dealer."

I blew on the tart and touched the crust with the tip of one finger. "I think it's okay now."

"Go ahead."

I picked it up and took a bite. The inside was so hot it burned my mouth. I started to cry.

"You are no better than a *gamin*," the pastry chef said, his voice suddenly cruel. "Your tongue is made of flesh and burns like an ordinary boy's."

One of the cooks brought me a cup of cold milk. "Shame on you," she said to the Pastry Chef. "The Queen will hear of this."

"What if she does?" he shrugged. "She has less power over me than my wife, who is a scullery maid."

I didn't want the tart anymore. "I think I'll go now," I said. But the stool was too high for me to get down by myself. "Could you please help me?" I asked.

"I would like nothing better than to take the Little Royal down," the Pastry Chef said. But he didn't move.

I looked at him so he would know I sincerely needed help, but he just sat there and grinned. I turned to face the stool and climbed down the rungs like a ladder, all the while afraid he would kick it off balance and I would crash to the floor.

I ran out of the kitchen and found Maman in her chamber, working on her embroidery. I threw myself into her arms and tried to tell her the Pastry Chef made me burn my tongue. But she thought I was crying because I didn't get to eat the tart. When I opened my mouth to explain, I vomited all over myself.

Maman gave me a bath and put me to bed. Papa and Marie were there, too.

"They're trying to poison us," Papa said.

"Why does the Pastry Chef want to poison me?" I asked.

"Because you're the Dauphin," Marie sniffed.

Maman gave her a harsh look. "Was that necessary?"

"We can't get rid of him," Papa said. "It would give the impression we don't trust our own citizens."

"We must have a Royal Taster again," Maman said.

"No," Papa shook his head. "They might send us an assassin instead."

After that, each of us carried a vial of almond oil around our necks, to take as an antidote in case we were poisoned. And we never ate anything we were served. When food was brought in from the palace kitchen, we lifted our forks, to appear as if we were about to eat.

As soon as the servants left the room, Madam Campan unlocked a cabinet and handed each of us a piece of bread and cold meat. We held the safe food in our laps and sneaked bites when the servants weren't looking. We mustn't let it touch the plates or it might get poison on it.

Madam Campan circled the table with a bucket, so we could dump the suspect food into it.

When a servant came in, she hid the bucket under her chair.

I could see all of this was hard on Papa because he loved to eat. Marie told me he couldn't control himself.

"He's the King," I corrected her. "He controls everything."

"First of all, not anymore," she replied smartly, "Secondly—King or Citizen—Papa can't control himself around food. He's a *glutton.*"

I could tell by the way she said it that Marie had learned the word *glutton* from the newspaper.

That winter, Maman's brother, Holy Roman Emperor Joseph II, died. Maman said he was poisoned.

"Does being a King mean your subjects are always trying to poison you?" I asked Marie.

"More or less."

all. She was never going to visit. He said this only to lure me into a dark room and taunt me with the promise of a visit that is never going to happen.

I pound on the door, willing to risk a beating as the price of being released from the Darkness. No one responds. I pound harder.

"Let me out. Please!" I cry. "Please, Reynard. I'll be very good if you would only open the door."

I pound and cry and plead until my throat is sore and my knuckles are bleeding. I lean against the door and slide down to the floor, whimpering like a scared puppy.

"Please let me out." My voice is a squeak in the infinite Darkness.

Reynard has played a dirty trick on me. I fell for it. I truly am the fool he says I am.

"You're as big a fool as your father," he often reminds me.

I wait for him to let me out and taunt me about how funny it was, the look on my face when he said I would be getting a visit from my sister.

I fear Reynard has gotten drunk and forgotten about me. Or fallen asleep. Or gone away.

I sing the "Carmagnole" at the top of my lungs, again and again, hoping it will either please or annoy him enough to get his attention.

In response, I get only silence.

3 years earlier . . .

Soon after my sixth birthday, Maman said we were going away for Easter.

She was so worn out from being hated so much that Papa thought she needed to get away from what he called the *epicenter*, to rest and recuperate. He walked across the Tuileries Garden to the Pavilion, an old horse-training ring where the National Assembly met, to ask permission for us to go on vacation.

When he returned, an hour later, Marie and I could tell by the way his shoulders drooped that he didn't get the answer he wanted.

He and Maman stepped into another room and spoke softly. Then they told us, "The trip has been delayed."

"*Delayed* means it's never going to happen," Marie, who was twelve, complained.

"That's enough out of you, Miss Smarty-pants," Maman said.

I began to understand that Papa wasn't exactly the King anymore. He was still the King. But not the kind of King who gets to have his way all the time. He had become the kind of King who has to ask permission from a hundred men to go anywhere or do anything. Like take his family on vacation. And their answer is always, No.

"Why can't Papa order everyone around and tell them what to do anymore?" I asked Marie.

"The National Assembly voted that the King doesn't have as much power as he used to," she explained. "Now he's a king with a *small k.*"

"He's the King. No one can tell him what to do," I reminded her. "Why doesn't he ignore them?"

"Because he's afraid."

"Afraid of what?"

"What do you think?" she smirked.

I couldn't imagine what Papa, who was a fearless hunter, could possibly be afraid of. I decided that I do not want to be the kind of King who is afraid of my own subjects.

The Road to Varennes
21 June 1791

A few weeks later, I awoke in a coach and six. Maman sat next to me, facing forward. Papa and Marie were on the bench across from us, facing backward. Papa was bent over with his face in his hands.

"Are we on holiday?" I asked.

"We're escaping," Marie said.

"That's enough, Miss Know-it-all," Maman snapped.

In fairy tales, you only need to escape when someone is trying to kill you.

"Are they going to murder us?" I asked.

I was more terrified to realize this idea had come to my mind so quickly than I was of the actual possibility that we could be murdered.

"Go to sleep." Maman said.

The coach stopped suddenly, tossing me to the floor at Papa's feet and smashing Marie's and Maman's foreheads into each other. Papa lifted his face from his hands and looked around, as if awoken from a dream.

The coachman appeared at the window. "Cracked wheel rim, your Majesty. I need everyone to step out, to take the weight off while I fix it."

Maman turned to Papa. "What if someone sees us?"

"It's dark. No one is on the road. And we're in disguise."

I then noticed that Papa was dressed like the head Gardener at Versailles. Maman and Marie were dressed like milkmaids. They must have gotten their outfits from the costume room of Maman's playhouse. I looked down at myself and saw that I was dressed like a stable boy.

Maman told Marie and me to hide in the wheat field. Papa walked slowly up the road. I ran to catch up and grabbed his hand.

"Louis," Maman whispered loudly to Papa. "Where are you going?"

"To see what we can see from the top of the hill," he said.

"Don't even think about it," Maman hissed to Marie.

I walked with Papa along the dirt road in the dim light from the moon that peeked through gray, shredded clouds. From the top of the hill, we saw a man walking beside a mule-drawn peddler's cart, making his way toward us.

"What do we do?" I whispered, prepared to run.

"Halloo!" Papa called out.

The peddler stopped next to us. "Dark night," he said.

I reached up to pet his mule's muzzle. "What's his name?"

"Louis."

I almost blurted out, "That's our name, too!"
But I covered my mouth to keep the words from
escaping.

"Where are you headed?" Papa asked.

"The village," the peddler answered. "And
you?"

"Varennes."

The peddler nodded and continued on,
passing our broken carriage without stopping. We
returned to find Maman and Marie hidden in the
wheat.

"What were you thinking?" Maman whispered
harshly.

"He didn't recognize me," Papa assured her.

"How do you know?"

"He would have bowed."

"At least you didn't tell him where we're
going," Maman sighed.

Papa was silent.

"You told him?"

Papa looked at his shoes.

"Honestly, Louis, sometimes you behave like a child who doesn't have the sense you were born with."

"He seemed like a nice enough fellow," Papa replied. "He wasn't wearing a cockade or red cap."

"You're too trusting, Louis. You're going to get us all killed."

"I'm still their King," he grumbled.

"Until he's not," Marie whispered in my ear.

By the time we reached the gates of Varennes, strands of peony-pink clouds were stretched across a custard yellow horizon.

"Where are they?" Maman asked.

"Where are who?" I asked.

"*Shhh*," Maman said to me. To Papa she said, "Three hundred Hussars were supposed to meet us here, to escort us across the border."

"They'll be here," Papa said.

"We're going across a *border*?" I asked. I wasn't sure what a *border* was, but it sounded like something you cross on the way to an adventure.

"What if we've been betrayed?" Maman said.

The gates screeched open. A squadron of National Guardsmen approached.

"They're wearing the *tricolour*," Maman whispered.

I recognized the plume of feathers—one red, one white, and one blue—that signaled a person's loyalty to the people who hate us.

"I knew I couldn't trust that new lady-in-waiting," Maman said bitterly.

Madam Campan had returned to her family farm after the Revolutionaries burned down her house in Paris.

An officer yelled at our driver, who yelled back.

"Seize him!" the officer commanded.

From inside the coach, it sounded as if they were pulling our driver from his perch.

"Are these the wicked men who are going to murder us?" I asked.

"Probably," Marie said.

I slid off my seat and crouched on the floor so no one could see me.

The officer opened the door. "Step out, Louis," he commanded.

I had never heard anyone who wasn't Maman call Papa "Louis." I had never heard anyone who isn't family call him anything but Your Majesty.

Papa lumbered out of the coach.

"You, too, Madam *Gabelle*. And the royal rats."

I expected Maman to tell Papa to tell the officer not to call us rats. Instead, she wrapped her shawl around her shoulders and stepped onto the muddy road. Marie followed. I lay on the carriage floor, very quiet.

"Where is the Dauphin?" the angry man demanded.

No one said anything. I didn't know if I should remain hiding or reveal myself. I was afraid if I stayed hidden, I would be left behind. That they would murder Maman and Papa and Marie, leaving me all alone. I decided I would rather be chopped up or shot down by canon with my family, than left to live without them.

It was the first important decision I had ever made all by myself.

"Here I am!" I said, jumping up from the floor.

I recognized the man standing next to the officer. The peddler with the mule named Louis.

"How did you know it was me?" Papa asked.

The peddler held up a coin from the Royal Mint, stamped with Papa's face in profile.

"I recognized your nose."

They made us ride back to Paris in a mail coach driven by Revolutionary soldiers. The officer and two others crowded inside. Papa held his face in his hands and said nothing. Maman squeezed me close to her side. One of the soldiers grinned stupidly at Marie, who crossed her arms across her chest and glared at him.

The newspapers called it our Failed Flight to Varennes. After that, the people distrusted Papa even more.

"If they hate us so much," I asked, "why won't they let us leave? Wouldn't they like to be rid of us?"

"They would like to be rid of us," Marie assured me. "But not by freeing us."

A man was accused of trying to help us escape. He was questioned with torture, but insisted the Royal family knew nothing of his scheme. For this, he was convicted of treason and beheaded by guillotine.

4

The Darkness
January 1794

I hear men's voices. I am relieved beyond measure. They pound on the door frame. I think they are Reynard's friends, determined to taunt me before letting me out.

Then I realize the sound is from hammers, nailing boards across the door.

They are sealing me in.

"No! . . . Please! . . . Don't leave me here!"

They add more and more boards, until I can barely hear them pounding. I feel nauseous. My heart pounds impatiently, like a bullfrog poised to jump free of my chest.

"I think I'm having a heart attack," I say.

Reynard is responsible for me. The Government Men would not be pleased if he left me to die.

I pound and beg and plead to be let out, until my voice is so hoarse, I can't speak above a whisper. My throat closes in on itself.

I lick my bleeding knuckles. The salty, metallic taste calms me. My breath evens out. The bullfrog crouches, awaiting the perfect moment to escape from its bone-and-flesh cage.

I suddenly realize I need to pee. I walk two steps. My shin bumps into something. A narrow wooden bed, low to the floor, with an edge, like a shallow box. There is no mattress, pillow, or blanket. Just a scattering of straw.

I feel around for a chamber pot. I'm not surprised there isn't one. At Versailles, there was a chamber pot in my bedchamber and a maid to dump it for me. Now I must choose a corner for going potty. I pick the one furthest from the door and the bed.

I feel ashamed, like a dog who pees on the rug and knows he's been bad.

I shiver and wrap my arms around myself. I am wearing only my sleeping shirt and linens. My toes are numb. I squeeze them in my palms to warm them.

Maman used to say, "If your lips are blue, it's time to come inside from playing in the snow." I can't see my lips. But they feel blue.

I sit in the dark a long, long time. Finally, I curl up on my side in the straw, placing my hands together under my cheek.

2 ½ years earlier . . .

The fall after I turned six, Papa agreed to
sign a Constitution. He brought Maman,
Marie, and me to the Pavilion across from the
Tuileries, to read his letter to the National
Assembly. Maman insisted that we not dress
up and try not to appear as if we thought we
were no better than the men in the room.

We stood inside the double doors. Maman
placed me in front of her, with her arms
draped over my shoulders, her hands clasped
at my chest. Marie, who was twelve, slouched
behind us.

Papa stood on a platform at the front and
read his letter. After every few words, the
Government Men interrupted with shouting
and yelling.

"Are they angry or cheering?" I asked.

"Cheering," Maman said.

"For now," Marie grumbled.

"Don't make things worse than they already are," Maman hissed.

"I don't see how they *could* be any worse," Marie mumbled.

"You see there my wife and children," Papa announced, "who honor the Constitution as sincerely as any Citizen."

Seven-hundred-and-fifty men twisted their necks to look at us. Maman was smiling her Royal Smile.

Someone shouted, *"Vive la Reine!"*

"Vive la Reine!" others echoed.

"Vive le Dauphin!"

I put on my Royal Smile. *Maybe if I smile hard enough,* I thought, *they will let us go home to Versailles.* I smiled so hard, my cheeks hurt.

"Vive la Princess!" they chanted.

Marie's mouth twisted into what Maman called her *sardonic* smile. Which was the opposite of a Royal Smile.

Papa lifted his pen. The room hushed, then went silent as he signed his name to the Constitution. I could hear the quill scratching across the paper. When he finished, the Assemblymen exploded into more chanting and cheering.

"Vive le Roi!"

"Vive le Roi!"

We walked back to the Tuileries, where a cheering mob was crowded into the garden and courtyard, chanting.

"Vive le Roi!"

« *Vive la constitution !* »

"Vive la liberté!"

Papa led us out the glass double-doors from the breakfast room onto the terrace. He was smiling for the first time since the night they dragged us away from Versailles. I wasn't sure if it was his Royal Smile or his regular smile. I wondered if they were the same thing for him.

Maman wore her Royal Smile like a masque at a costume ball.

Marie stood scowling, with her arms across her chest.

"At least wave," Maman told her.

"For months, they've wanted to kill us," Marie reasoned. "Now we're supposed to believe they want us to live long lives?"

Maman grabbed Marie's wrist, yanked it high over her head, and moved it back and forth, as if Marie were a marionette and Mama was pulling her strings. It was supposed to look like a waive, but Marie's fist was clenched.

At supper, Papa was jubilant. He ate stacks of pastries baked fresh by the Revolutionary Chef. "We no longer have to worry about being poisoned," he said. Crumbs sprayed from his mouth and fell from his lips onto his chest.

When the servants left the room, Maman said, "These people want no sovereigns."

"I have signed their Constitution. Everything is resolved," Papa said, cramming so much food into his mouth, he had to chew with it open.

"Until it's not," Marie said.

"What does the Constitution do?" I asked.

"It strips the King of nearly all his power," Maman said bitterly. "This won't be the end of it. They have commanded us to hand them the crown jewels. They are demolishing the monarchy, stone by stone."

"We're still here, aren't we?" Papa said.

The mob remained all night, cheering and chanting. People in revolutionary cockades tossed flowers onto the terrace. Military bands played marching music. Celebratory cannonballs were shot from the bridges. Fireworks exploded over the Seine.

I decided when I become King, I will sign a constitution, so my subjects will celebrate me with fireworks and cannons. And wish my family a long life.

Three months after my seventh birthday, the cheers died down and the mean chants started up again.

"Why are they angry again?" I asked, one morning at breakfast.

"They no longer want a King *and* a Constitution, like the English," Maman said. "They want *no king at all*, like the Americans."

Papa commanded his Swiss Guards not to shoot, if the crowd were to force their way into the courtyard.

"I will lose my head before I fire on my own subjects," he said.

Maman spoke to Marie and me in German, which Papa couldn't understand. "I am the daughter of Holy Roman Emperor Francis I and of Maria Theresia, Queen of Hungary and Bohemia. My brothers were the Holy Roman

60

Emperors Joseph II and Leopold II. My nephew is Holy Roman Emperor Francis II," she reminded us. "My family can save us from this Revolution by sending Austrian troops into Paris. But your father refuses to accept their aid."

I guess Papa understood enough of what she had said, because he declared, "I am King of France. I shall never shed a single drop of French blood. Speak no more of it."

Just then, five angry men and women burst into the room. Papa stood abruptly, his napkin falling from his lap. Globs of raspberry jam stuck to the corners of his mouth.

"What do you want?" he asked.

A woman held out a red cap with blue and white feathers.

"Wear the Red Cap of Liberty for all to see," she demanded.

Papa grabbed my hand. Maman grabbed my other hand. Papa led us through the glass doors onto the terrace. A sea of people in red caps had forced their way past the guard posts into the courtyard.

"*Le pain se lève!*" they chanted. "The bread will rise!"

Papa looked out over the crowd. They hushed, expecting him to make a statement. But he said nothing.

Marie and I exchanged glances. Even I knew his failure to speak was cowardly and shameful.

A woman behind him placed the Red Cap of Liberty on his head. It was too small, so he held it in place with his hand. The people cheered.

The woman tried to place a red cap on Maman's head, saying, "Your turn, Madam Deficit."

Maman grabbed it out of her hand. This made the mob unhappy. They boo-ed and hissed and chanted. "Death to Madam Veto!"

Then Maman placed the red cap on *my* head. It was too big and covered my eyes.

The mob cheered, *"Vive le Dauphin!"*

I waved, which made them cheer even louder, which made me smile. I wasn't sure if it was my Royal Smile or my regular smile.

We stepped back from the balcony. With the glass doors closed, the chanting was muffled. The people who had interrupted our breakfast wandered out. When the last person was gone, Papa tore the red cap from his head and threw it into the fireplace.

I was not sure if I wanted to remove my red cap, which made the mob love me. I wondered why Maman refused to wear it, if all she had to do to make them stop hating her was place it on her head.

I continued to wear my Red Cap of Liberty through supper. When no one was looking, I hid it under my mattress. When I am King, I thought, I

will take it out and wear it again, so my people
will not hate me.

After I wore the Red Cap of Liberty,
Maman was especially strict about letting me
go out on the terrace. She wanted me to play
inside, always at her feet.

"Stay close enough that I can grab you and
run if I need to," she said.

"But I'm seven now," I protested.

"It's too dangerous," she snapped.

"Why do the angry people call Maman the
Austrian Swine?" I asked Marie later.

She was thirteen and no longer read the
newspapers on the floor. Now she sat next to
Papa, who handed her each page after he read
it.

"Maman was born in Austria and spoke German before she spoke French," she explained. "The French hate her accent. They see her as a foreigner and believe she is a spy for the Austrian government."

"Is she?" I asked.

"A spy?"

I nodded.

"Why wouldn't she be?" Marie shrugged.

This was the type of question Marie sometimes asked that left me feeling there was a mystery or secret message inside her words. But I couldn't break the code.

"Is that why she tells everyone she can't remember a word of German, but speaks it to us when no one is around?"

"Obviously."

"Why do they call her Madam Deficit?"

"They think she spends too much money on clothes and jewels and banquets for herself and her friends. And leaves nothing for the French people."

"What does *the bread will rise* mean?"

"When you put a loaf of bread in the oven, it rises. Right?"

"Yeah."

"The people are saying that they are like bread and will rise up in protest. Also, because they are starving for bread."

"That doesn't make sense."

"No," she agreed. "But it gets your attention."

5

The Darkness
January 1794

They have carved a slit out of the bottom of
the door and installed a rotating circular board,
like the Lazy Susan on our banquet table at
Versailles. The circle is divided by upright boards
into four sections. From their side, they place a tin
plate in one section, then spin it halfway, so it
appears on my side. I can hear them lock the tray
in place with a padlock.

I sit on the floor with my back against the wall
and the plate on my lap. My fingers dip into a bowl

of murky bracken. It reminds me of our visit to Normandy, which I have ruled as Duke since the day I was born. I was very young, maybe three. As I played in the sand, clumps of seaweed washed ashore in golden-brown tangles. I grabbed a handful and shoved it into my mouth. At first it tasted salty. Then it tasted green. Then it tasted foul and fishy. I tried to spit it out, but it wouldn't go away. I stood on the beach and wailed.

My bowl of so-called soup tastes worse than rotting seaweed.

Next, my fingers come across a pile of mush. I pinch a clump between my thumb and forefinger and taste it with the tip of my tongue. It has crunchy bits, dried beans or lentils, soaked in luke-warm water.

Three round things roll around on the plate. I pick one up and bite into it. A chestnut. Raw, tough, and bitter, not roasted and sprinkled with salt, like we used to eat at Christmas.

For the first time in my life, I understand the importance of salt to make food edible. Papa used to grumble about the salt tax, called the *gabelle*. He said the people were unhappy with the *gabelle*, that it was so high they could not afford to buy salt for their cooking. I remember him quoting from a newspaper, "The tax on salt costs more than the salt."

One of the insults the mobs used to call out to Maman was Madam *Gabelle*. I thought at the time that the people might easily do without salt, if the price did not please them. But now, faced with a meal entirely devoid of salt, I understand their unhappiness.

Did the people who cheered when Papa's head was cut off want him to lower the tax on salt? And, if so, couldn't he have lowered it? Was his profit from the *gabelle* worth the cost of his head? Papa vowed he would lose his head before he would shed French blood. But was it necessary to lose his head over a salt tax?

I wish Marie were here to explain it all. Or to shove a newspaper in my face, call me an *idiot*, and tell me to figure it out on my own.

I vow that, when my troubles are over and I am allowed to reign as King of France, I will ban the *gabelle*. Forever.

1 ½ years earlier . . .

The summer after my seventh birthday, we were moved to the Temple Tower, in a different section of the city, where we were crammed into three connected rooms on the ground floor. Three guards were posted within our living space, three more outside the door, and a dozen surrounding the Tower.

"This Temple used to be the home of the Knights Templar," Papa told me. "The brave men who went on Crusade in the Holy Land."

Maman had read me many adventure tales of the Knights Templar, in books illuminated with colored drawings framed in gold leaf. I was excited beyond belief to be living in their castle.

"The furniture is falling apart. Everything is covered in dust. The whole place smells musty," Maman complained. "It's positively Medieval."

"It's no palace," Papa admitted.

"What do you expect in a royal prison-house?" Marie said.

"Are we in prison?" I asked.

"See what you've started?" Maman said to Marie.

"I need a sword," I told Papa, "for slaying dragons."

Papa carved a wooden sword from the leg of an old table. But Maman and Papa were not happy living in the Temple.

"Don't be sad, Maman," was all I could think to say. "Don't be sad, Papa."

They smiled in a sad way.

"I'll protect you from the dragons," I assured them.

They laughed and hugged me close. Later, I learned that a sad smile is better than no smile.

The Tower
December 1792

Each morning, Papa was taken by coach to the Assembly Hall, where his trial was being held.

"What's a trial?" I asked.

"It's where the National Convention will decide your Papa's fate," Maman said.

"What's fate?"

"Fate is what is going to happen to you in the future, no matter how hard you try to change it," Marie explained.

"Why isn't Papa like the kings in fairytales? The ones who can make everyone do whatever they want?"

"The Revolutionaries voted him out of power," Marie said.

Maman gave her a mean look. Then she shook her head, as if giving up on ever stopping Marie from telling me things I wasn't supposed to know.

I dressed in my Swiss Guards uniform and patrolled the Temple battlements with Marie. Maman said Marie, who had just turned fourteen, would have to start behaving like a lady.

"When I was your age," Maman told her, "I was married to your father, who was fifteen. We were wed by proxy, before we even met. He spoke no German and I could barely speak French. By eighteen and nineteen, we were reigning as King and Queen of France."

"Why did you get married, if you didn't know each other?" Marie asked.

"Austria and France had been at war a long time. Our parents thought by marrying an Austrian princess to a French prince, our countries would remain friends. Now they call me the Austrian Swine. As if it's all my fault."

"That sounds like a terrible idea," Marie said, crossing her arms over her chest, as if Maman was about to make her marry a foreign prince right then and there.

"Okay, Madam Spinster," Maman said. "*You* go ahead and solve Europe's diplomatic problems. *You* try to stop another thirty-year war."

"I think we need to stop a Revolution first," Marie smirked.

Maman pretended not to hear her.

"Will Louis be forced to marry a foreign princess?" Marie asked.

"He will marry a princess," Maman replied. "But she will not be foreign. Not if I have any say. I would not wish on any girl the loneliness and hatred I've endured. I was made to leave my mother at fifteen and never saw her again."

I thought about the princesses in fairy tales, the drawings of girls in pointy hats with pink gauze flowing from them, standing atop towers like the Temple, their arms flung up in distress. Then I thought of Lisette, the Gardener's daughter, who I used to play with at Versailles.

Marie, who could sometimes read my mind, said, "The Dauphin wants to marry the Gardener's daughter."

"No, I don't," I said.

Even though we were already married.

Papa came home each evening so worn down by his trial, he could barely hug me. At supper, he ate excessively. Like a *glutton*.

Maman looked at him the way she looked at me when I had a high fever. Our meals were so tense, Marie and I kicked each other under the table.

"Why do the people call Papa the Sleeping Rhinoceros?" I asked, to break the silence.

Earlier that day, Marie had shown me a newspaper illustration of a fat, slumbering beast with a horned snout, wearing a crown.

Maman's face shut down. Papa kept eating.

"Because," Marie explained later, "he has a big, pointy nose, like the horn of a rhino." Then she added, "And because he is lazy and does nothing."

"He's not lazy," I argued. "He used to go hunting every day and returned with dozens of carcasses."

"Exactly," she said.

When I am King, I vowed to myself, I will not be lazy and do nothing.

But how will I know what to do?

One afternoon, Papa came back from his trial early. His face was grim.

He and Maman went into their chambers, where they play whist late at night. Then they called us in to join them.

Papa held me close. "My sweet boy. After tomorrow, I shall never lay eyes on you again."

I had only ever seen him cry once before. When my brother, the first Dauphin, died.

"Papa, no!" Marie wailed. "How can they do this to you? They are your subjects. They ought to love you."

Papa shook his head in wonderment. "I have agreed to all of their demands. They asked for a meeting of the Estates General and I called it. They wished to reconfigure the government and name themselves the National Assembly, and I consented. They wished me to sign their

Constitution, and I signed it. I have never once raised my voice against them."

"You've done everything you could," Maman said, patting his arm. "Short of accepting military aid from your friends, to put down this heinous rebellion."

"King George III went to war against his own subjects in the American colonies, turning cousin against cousin, killing thousands of English citizens," Papa said. "The English King Charles I responded to his unruly Parliament by dismissing them. What did that get him? Years of civil war and a fine beheading."

Maman ran into her bedchamber, holding her handkerchief to her mouth. Marie followed her.

Papa stood me in front of him with his hands on my shoulders and looked me straight in the eyes. "When I am gone, you will become King," he said gravely.

I wanted to cry. But I could see he had more to say. That these were to be the most important words I would ever hear from his lips.

"No matter what happens," he continued, speaking as one man to another, "do not seek revenge against those who have orchestrated my demise."

"I don't understand."

"There are men over there," he gestured with his head to the National Assembly Hall, "who wish to abolish the House of Bourbon, though we have ruled France for hundreds of years. Promise me you will not seek vengeance against them."

"Against who, Papa?"

"Against the Revolutionaries. Against the National Assembly. Or whatever they decide to call themselves. Against the regicides. Against the French people. They truly believe they're doing what's best for France. When you are King, never seek to punish those who have wronged us."

"But you are my father and the King of France. I must defend your honor at all costs."

"No, my darling son." Papa stood up. "Promise me you will never seek vengeance in my name. You must never shed French blood."

I solemnly promised, though I didn't understand the significance of his words.

The next morning, the National Guardsmen came to take Papa away.

"Please," I begged, pulling at their uniforms. "Don't murder my Papa. He is a good King. He said yes to everything you wanted. He signed your Constitution. He never raised his voice against a French citizen. He never spilled a single drop of French blood."

Inside the coach, Papa sat with his face in his hands. Marie wrapped her arms around my shoulders and turned me back to the royal prison house.

All of Paris came out to watch as Papa was driven to the Guillotine. I stood on the Temple turret with Maman and Marie. A river of red caps filled the streets, pouring down the boulevards, and converging into a sea of red at the *Place de la Révolution*.

I knew the moment Papa was beheaded, because Maman fell to her knees and hailed me as King Louis XVII. She anointed me with three drops of jasmine perfume, rubbed into my hair.

"Where's my crown?" I asked.

I was seven years old, and it seemed a perfectly reasonable question at the time. Now that I'm eight, I see what a fool I was for asking. Marie must have been smirking behind my back.

I had only ever seen the royal crown in paintings of Papa's coronation. Maman explained that the crown, along with the royal jewels, used to be kept at the Cathedral in Reims, where Bourbon coronations had been held for hundreds of years. But the Revolutionaries demanded that the crown and royal jewels be handed over to the people of France.

The mobs filling the streets, who should have been chanting, *"Vive le roi!"* in my honor, were chanting, *"Le roi est mort!"*

"Everyone says he was a bad King," Marie cried. "But what they don't understand is, he was the best Papa in the world!"

Back in our rooms, Maman and Marie sat on the edge of Maman's bed, their arms around each other, foreheads touching. I felt as distressed and sad as they were, but my face wouldn't cry. I had gotten all my crying out when they put Papa in the carriage that morning.

I knew he was dead. His head had been sliced off by a giant blade they call the National Razor. But I couldn't make my mind believe he would never come back.

All night, canons were fired over the Seine to celebrate the execution of King Louis XVI. Drums beat out military marches. Fireworks hissed and popped over the city.

Marie read in the morning paper that Papa's last words were, "What have I done wrong?"

I wished I could understand what made his subjects want to chop off his head—so that, when they let me rule in my rightful place as their King, I will know what *not* to do.

The angry people had spent a lot of time shouting about bread. Maman said there are plenty of other things to eat. But I still didn't understand why Papa didn't give them enough flour to keep them from voting to execute him.

"When I rule as King," I told Marie. "I will make sure everyone in France has enough bread to eat."

"It's not that simple," she said, hugging me to her side.

"Yes, it is!" I sobbed. Because it was much too late to give the people so much bread that they would reattach Papa's horn-nosed head to his corpulent body.

6

The Darkness
Winter 1794

I think of myself as Robinson Crusoe, from the first book I read all by myself. The lone survivor of a shipwreck, Crusoe is stranded on a desert island. He names it The Island of Despair.

Instead of laying around on the beach crying his eyes out and hoping a ship will come to save him, Crusoe employs his time with *industry*. He hunts and forages. He writes a diary on dried leaves with ink made from berry juice. He scratches out a calendar on the wall of a cave. He builds a shelter with palm fronds. He sews clothing from animal skins, using a needle made of bone.

At least, that's how I remember the story.

But Robinson Crusoe was luckier than I am. He lived on a tropical island. He watched the sunset over the ocean. He felt the warmth of its rays on his cheeks. He heard the breeze rustling in the trees. He squished sand between his toes. He listened to birds singing and monkeys chattering and the roar of waves crashing to shore. He swam with friendly dolphins and ate fresh lobster grilled over an open flame.

I am cut off from all light and sound and feel nothing on my toes but cold, dank stone.

One of the first things Robinson Crusoe does is explore his surroundings. I walk from one corner of my Island of Darkness at a diagonal to the opposite corner, crossing it in three paces. I cross between the other two corners, then from one wall to the opposite wall in rows, like a farmer plowing a field.

There is absolutely nothing here but the bed and a scattering of straw.

I examine every stone of my chamber. My fingertips are my eyes. I pull the bed to one corner and stand on it, reaching up as high as I can. I imagine I am an apprentice mason, who will one day have to build a castle for my King, and that I must study the size, shape and layout of every block of stone in the Temple Tower.

Maybe I will find a hidden passageway. Or a loose block. Or a forgotten treasure. For a moment, I fear I will come across the skeleton of a boy, the previous prisoner of the Darkness.

I run my hands over each block, starting as high as I can reach, working my way down to the floor, then moving the bed and beginning again at the top. The lowest bricks are the coldest. They grow gradually warmer, the higher they rise.

At the very lowest block in the last corner, I feel a chink in the stone. I stick my hand in to find out how deep it goes. Something grabs my finger in its teeth. I scream and yank my hand out. I suck on my finger, tasting blood.

A rat.

"Stupid rat! Keep your teeth to yourself."

I gather straw from the bed and cram it into the hole to block it up. I stay on the bed frame with my feet off the floor.

I lay awake, listening to the squeaking of the rat as he runs in the walls. I fear he will nibble through the straw, climb up the leg of the bed, and gnaw on my toes. Or bite chunks out of my eyeballs, as if they are juicy grapes.

If I feel myself drifting off, I wake myself up again. I must remain vigilant.

The rat is standing on my chest. I can't see his eyes, but I feel him staring at me with his night vision. If I don't move a muscle, maybe I won't scare him into biting me.

He crawls toward my face and sniffs my mouth. I gasp and hold my breath. His whiskers tickle my nostrils. He scurries down one leg of the bed and back into his nook.

Something warm and fuzzy is pressed against my belly. The rat has crawled under the hem of my shirt and curled up next to me as I lay on my side.

He must be cold, and I'm the warmest place he can find. He makes me feel a less cold, too. The tiny exhale of his breath helps me fall asleep and the rhythm of his little rat snores comforts my dreams.

Day after day, I yell through the slot, at whoever delivers my plate, to have mercy on me. To speak to me. To let me out. To tell me how long I've been here. And how long they intend to keep me here.

In response, I get only silence.

When you're alone in the dark with no one to talk to, time crawls as slowly as a dying cockroach.

1 year earlier . . .

After Papa was beheaded, Maman, Marie, and I were confined to a single room on the third floor of the Tower.

Maman sat on the stool, working on her embroidery and humming German folk songs. Marie, who had turned fifteen in December, and I were not allowed books to study, or quills or paper, because the Government Men were afraid we would pay the guards to smuggle escape plans to our allies. So Maman gave us thread to play Cat's Cradle. We played patty-cake and sang *"Frère Jacques,"* even though we had outgrown these silly games.

I thought my eighth birthday, my first as King Louis XVII, would go down in history as the worst of my entire life.

"I have nothing to give you," Maman cried.

"It's okay, Maman. I still love you. I wish Papa were here, though."

"I wish he were here, too," she said.

Marie glared into empty space and said nothing, as if she were scheming to kill someone. I feared she might stab one of the guards with Maman's sewing scissors.

I had been King of France for about three months.

Marie and I were sitting on the floor, playing with dominoes one of the guards had given us, and Maman was working on her embroidery, when three soldiers barged in without knocking. Maman was so startled she dropped her needle.

"The Little Capet must be separated from the Royal Wench," the officer announced.

Maman snatched me off the floor into her arms.

"No!" she screamed. "You cannot take my little boy!"

I was afraid of the guards. I did not want to be taken away. But most of all, I was embarrassed that Maman was treating me like a baby in front of strangers. It's not becoming of a King to be clasped in his mother's arms in front of his subjects.

"Orders from the Incorruptible," the officer said.

The man they call the Incorruptible is Maximilien Robespierre, head of the Committee of Public Safety and the most powerful man in France.

One of the soldiers grabbed Maman's arm. She yanked out of his grasp, squeezing me so tight it hurt.

"NO! NO! NO! NO! NO!"

Maman screamed and screamed. Marie sat in the corner with her eyes closed, plugging her ears with her fingers and rocking herself back and forth like a dull-witted child.

Two soldiers grabbed Maman while the third tried to pry me out of her arms. I hugged her neck as tightly as I could.

"Have mercy!" Maman said. "What if this were your own little boy?"

"My boy ain't a little King," the officer smirked.

"My Louis has done no wrong. He is innocent of any crime," Maman insisted.

The soldiers stood back, looking at each other uncertainly.

"He said not to hurt the Wolf Cub," one of them said.

I knew Maman was frightened, because she didn't order them to refer to me as His Majesty.

"How are we supposed to separate them, without hurting them?" another asked.

"He didn't say we can't hurt the Austrian Bitch," the third commented.

"Don't call Maman wicked names!" I yelled.

They looked at me, as if surprised I was capable of speech.

"How old is he?" the officer asked.

"I'm eight."

"Come with us, then."

"Are you taking me to the guillotine?"

"No! No! No!" Maman repeated, her voice hoarse from screaming.

This went on for a very long time. I was getting more and more upset by all the yelling and screaming and kisses and tears.

Finally, I said, "Maman, please stop yelling. You're hurting my ears."

"My dear, sweet, little boy. Will you be brave for me and go with these men?"

"Yes, Maman."

She kissed me on the cheeks and forehead and let go of me. As the soldiers were leading me out, she called, "Wait!"

They stopped in the doorway but kept their backs to her.

No one is ever supposed to turn their back to the King or Queen. At Versailles, I had seen people walk backwards away from Papa, down a long hallway, all the while in danger of stumbling or banging into something. Once, a servant walking backwards collided with a maid walking forward, carrying a pot of hot coffee.

Maman grabbed her sewing scissors, cut off a lock of her hair, wrapped it around her finger, opened the locket that hung from her neck, placed her hair in it, and closed it. Then she cut the ribbon shorter, retied it, and hung it around my neck. A miniature of Papa was painted on the front.

"Look at me," she commanded the guards.

They spun on their heels. The habit of obeying your Queen is hard to break. Even for revolutionary soldiers.

"I place a curse on anyone who tries to remove this locket from my boy's neck," she croaked.

Maman is no witch or sorceress. I had never before heard her cast a curse upon anyone—except Marie's cat, when it peed on her bed. But everyone takes a curse seriously, no matter whose lips utter it. Even a hated foreign Queen. Maybe especially a hated foreign Queen.

The soldiers escorted me a flight of stone steps to a room exactly the same as the one we had been living in for half a year. It had a narrow bed with a thin straw mattress, a small table and chair, and a hearth. A slit of a window looked out over the park through iron bars.

An old man in laborer's clothes sat on a low, three-legged stool, smoking a pipe.

"The Royal Capet is all yours," the officer said. The men were glad to be rid of me. I was certain their ears were still ringing from all the screaming, because mine were, too.

The old man told me his name was Reynard and that he was a shoemaker and a member of the Paris Commune.

"What's the Paris Commune?"

"A group of men that rules Paris," he explained grumpily. He was the type of adult who doesn't like to be asked questions. "And none of us is aristocracy," he added.

When he said the word "aristocracy," he spat a brown, watery mass onto the floor. I cringed, afraid I might step in it with my bare feet. Maman told me spit carries diseases.

"My mission is to turn you from an aristocrat," Reynard said, spitting, "into a Revolutionary."

Reynard's first lesson was to make me sing the "Carmagnole." He pulled me out of bed in the middle of the night and placed the Red Cap of Liberty on my head, yanking it down tight so that it covered my eyes. He and three of his friends sat in a circle on stools and overturned buckets, passing around a bottle of wine.

"The 'Carmagnole' cannot be sung correctly if one is not inebriated," they explained.

They grabbed me by the hair, wrenched my head back, and poured wine into my mouth until it ran down my chin. I gagged and spit it onto my shirt.

Reynard ordered me to dance in crazy circles around them as they yelled out the lyrics to the "Carmagnole," demanding that I repeat them, word for word.

Marie Antoinette tried to knock us on our arses.
But she fell on her face and broke her nose.

They ordered me to weave in and out among them, prancing and skipping behind one man's back, in front of the next man, behind the man after that, and so on, until I spun and stumbled and lost my balance. Each time I fell, they grabbed me by the hair and pulled me up.

Go, Louis, you big cry baby,
Cry all the way from the Tuileries
To the Temple
To the Guillotine

Each time I sang a verse, they ordered me to sing the next one louder. And the one after that even louder. Until I was shouting so loud my throat burned.

When the Austrian Whore saw her
  prison
She wanted to turn back.

I felt dizzy and nauseous. I could not say the words to the last two lines without sobbing.

Madam Deficit was sick at heart
To see her husband shit himself.

Reynard made me start from the beginning and sing it all over again until I could say the line about Maman being "sick at heart" without choking on the words.

They made me sing the "Carmagnole" so many times, all I could think about when I tried to make myself sleep were the terrible words I had yelled about Maman and Papa. I wondered if Maman and Marie had heard me in their cell.

Reynard liked to play fetch. He would toss the Red Cap of Liberty into a corner. I was ordered to run on my hands and knees, retrieve the cap in my mouth, and carry it back to him. My bare knees were scraped raw against the stone floor.

One day, he told me the tombs of the former kings and queens, which lay in the Saint-Denis Basilica, had been dug up and their bodies roasted and eaten by the starving masses.

I didn't know whether to believe him or not. Maman once took me to Saint-Denis when I was little. All of the French royalty, dating back a thousand years, were buried there. Each king and queen had their own sarcophagus with a marble statue laid out over the top.

I was certain Papa's remains had not been laid to rest there, that he was given no sarcophagus or statue. Marie had read in the news months earlier that all the royal statues of Papa that once stood in the public parks and plazas had been torn down and melted to make canons for the Revolution.

Reynard brought me a mechanical canary that sang the "Carmagnole" when you wound it up. I threw it to the floor and stamped on it. Even though I knew he would beat me for being ungrateful.

7

The Darkness,
Spring 1794

An army of lice plays King of the Mountain on my scalp. My skin is itchy and scabby all over.

It must be Spring because I've stopped shivering and the stones are warmer. Which means I have probably turned nine by now.

Every night the rat snuggles against my belly. When I awaken, he is gone. (I can't know whether it's day or night. Or if a day has passed. Or three or ten days. Each time I wake up, I pretend it's a new day. Each time I lie down to sleep, I pretend it's night.)

I set a chestnut on the floor outside his hole and coax him with gentle words until he runs out, grabs it in his teeth and scurries back. After a few days of placing nuts further and further from his nook, he is eating out of my hand.

"You need a name," I tell him. "I bet you're going to have lots of adventures in the walls and nooks and crannies of the Temple."

Then it comes to me. "Your name is Alexander the Great."

Alexander the Great nestles in the crook of my neck, his silky tail stretched along the curve of my shoulder, his whiskers tickling my ear. I feel his twitchy little nose as he whispers soothing words only we can understand.

I know Alexander is young, because I feel him growing bigger and heavier in my hands with each passing day. If he had a Maman and Papa of his own, why would he be licking my cheek to say hello and eating chestnuts from my hand?

"Maybe your parents were poisoned," I tell him. "And you were left alone in the dark."

"Yes," he whispers. "The Green-eyed Monster murdered my parents and I was left to fend for myself."

I am not crazy. I know rats can't talk. But Alexander is smart. And he has feelings.

"You are a pearl, buried in manure," he tells me. "One day you will dig your way out and shimmer in the sunlight."

6 months earlier . . .

"We need evidence," Maximilien Robespierre barked, unfurling an official looking parchment.

The Green-Eyed Monster was a slight, pale man in a velvet frock and silk waistcoat with a frilly jabot. He wore spectacles with round lenses tinted lime green. He began to read, his voice sharp as a blade.

"The deposed King Louis XVI . . . The deposed Queen Marie Antoinette . . . The debased Dauphin . . ."

The document said terrible things about Maman. And yet, just hearing the names of my Maman and Papa spoken aloud, even by a monster, caused a bloom of warmth to spread in my chest.

"Marie Antoinette. . .," the Green-eyed Monster continued, in a dry, heartless tone, "counter-revolutionary activities . . . debauching the young prince . . . betraying the French people . . . treasonous intent . . . conspiring with the Spanish King . . . seeking to help the Dauphin escape . . . refusing to admit to her many crimes against the French people. . .."

I wanted to tell the Government Men that they were wrong. That Maman is a good person. Then I remembered the mobs of thousands who called her the Austrian Swine. Madam Deficit. Madam Veto. And how they threatened to strangle her with her own intestines. To roast and eat her liver. And how I begged them to forgive her, but they wouldn't listen.

Robespierre lay the parchment on the table. "Read your statement aloud."

"This isn't my statement," I said. "This is your statement."

The Green-eyed Monster smacked the side of my head with the back of his hand. Snot oozed down my nostrils onto my upper lip. I wiped my nose on the sleeve of my shirt. I dared not ask for a handkerchief. At Versailles, Maman carried blue silk handkerchiefs, embroidered with fleurs-de-lis in gold thread, tucked into the sleeve of her dress.

"Read," the Green-eyed Monster growled. Cruelty fumed from his pores like bile-green smoke.

I looked at the first words. I did not know them. I was once a good reader. My tutor Moses told me so. But I had not been allowed a tutor or book since our Failed Flight to Varennes.

"I . . ." I stuttered.

The Green-eyed Monster read the first part of the first sentence aloud, then made me repeat it. He continued through the document, reading one phrase at a time, waiting for me to repeat it, then going on to the next. When he read a lie about Maman, and I refused to say the words, he punched the back of my head, so hard my eyes watered and I felt nauseous.

After that, I repeated every word exactly and promptly. When we reached the end and I had spoken aloud terrible lies about Maman that made me feel ashamed, the Green-Eyed Monster dipped a quill in a pot of ink and handed it to me.

"Sign your name to confirm that these statements are true and verified and made by you without coercion."

I stared at the wicked document that was full of lies. I knew I must sign. But I could not lift my hand to take the quill.

"Sign, you *Royal Foetus!*" He screamed in my ear.

I tried to remember how Moses taught me to hold a pen. How to position my thumb and forefinger to keep it steady. How to press steadily on the paper, not so soft that I left gaps in my letters. But not so hard that I poked holes in the parchment.

I was certain I was signing my own death warrant. I wondered what Marie would say if they tried to make her sign such a document. Or if she already had. I feared if I refused to sign, Robespierre would punch me in the head until I passed out. Marie had said the people believed the Guillotine was merciful. Now I hoped they were right.

Hiding under the carriage seat at the gates of Varennes, only five years old, I had chosen to be murdered with my family rather than survive on my own. Now that I was eight, I had inside me an urgent will to live. Even with Papa dead. With Maman and Marie awaiting I knew not what fate.

My whole body was shaking as I touched quill to paper. The Government Men stared at my trembling hand, as if they believed something incredible was about to happen.

"You needn't compose a masterpiece."

"What name should I sign?"

I knew he would not like if I signed King Louis XVII.

"Louis-Charles Capet," he said impatiently.

I wrote slowly, in neat letters, fearful of being hit if I made a mistake, and blew on the ink to help it dry. Papa kept a cannister of powder on his desk, to dry the ink after he signed official documents. But I dared not ask for such a luxury. I was certain they would tell me powders are the stuff of foreign queens and treasonous kings.

The Tower
16 October 1793

The next day, Reynard's friends brought me a toy guillotine and a wooden doll, dressed as the Queen, with silver-blond hair coifed in a high tower, like Maman's. They demonstrated how Maman lay on her tummy on the board, how the executioner cut her hair to expose her neck. Then they made me pull the string that released the blade. It clunked down on the doll's neck. The wooden head fell into a basket.

"She's a head shorter than she used to be."

"A permanent cure for the Queen's headache."

"The national barber has given her a close shave."

They laughed and made me do it again. And again.

I knew they were lying. Maman was still in the cell above me. I could sense her there, whispering through the walls, the murmur of her voice reverberating in the ancient stones.

"You will never be King," Reynard assured me.

"I *am* the King!" I shouted. "I am King Louis XVII!"

Reynard punched me so hard, I was sent sprawling across the floor. One of my teeth was knocked loose and stuck in my throat. I coughed to dislodge it but ended up swallowing it.

"You are King Turd," Reynard declared.

8

The Darkness
Summer 1794

The air has changed from dank and chilly to warm and stuffy. I am nauseated by the build-up of my own poop, spilling out from the corner into the center of the room.

At Versailles, each bedroom had a carved wooden cabinet, the height of a low stool, inlaid with mother-of-pearl and gold floral designs. On top of the cabinet was a hole, lined with a smooth ring of silver that was cold on my bum on winter mornings. Inside the cabinet was a porcelain chamber pot, hand painted with miniature scenes of Chinese men in robes and long, drooping mustaches, walking over arched foot bridges and feeding koi fish in a pond with storks wading in the shallows.

I never thought about where all the poop and pee that filled my chamber pot each day went, after the maid took it away. I never wondered how awful it must have smelled. I never speculated as to where it was dumped or how long it stayed there.

Now I would like to go back in time and thank her for taking it away, so I could live in rooms perfumed with rose water and fresh cut lilies.

The gardens of Versailles were suffused with aromas of honeysuckle, jasmine, and lily of the valley. Roasting meat from the outdoor kitchen was always in the air. Rabbit. Boar. Venison. Partridge. Pheasant. Duck. The sweet, buttery aromas of tarts and croissants and baguettes and sourdough bread, fresh baked in a giant oven.

Maman collected perfumes from the East in multi-colored crystal bottles. Her vanity table was crowded with jars of makeup smelling of jonquil, carnation, hyacinth, and orange blossom. Her jade perfume dispenser was guarded by turquoise Chinese dragons. Her *pot-pourris* and jewelry cases and cabinets wafted hints of bergamot, lavender, rosemary, and violets. Leaving for the Opera, she playfully fluttered a sandalwood-scented fan in my face, her kid gloves scented with rose.

It's funny that things I used to hate, I now wish for.

"Why must I take baths?" I used to complain to Maman.

"Because you are a stinky little Duke," she would say. "Your grandmama can smell you all the way from Vienna."

Now I daydream about a warm, soapy bath. At Versailles, Maman had a deep copper bathtub. Maids carried cauldrons of hot water from the kitchen. A white lace curtain that hung from the ceiling wrapped around it, enclosing you in a steamy cocoon. Maman poured rosewater and jasmine oil into the water. When I got out, she told me I smelled "fresh as a daisy."

Another thing I used to think of as a chore, that I now miss dearly, were my lessons with Moses. He was from Berlin and called himself a Man of the Enlightenment. He took me to our rooftop terrace one night, where Papa had a telescope.

"See that yellow ball?" he asked, pointing to the sky. "That's Saturn."

"All I see are lots of stars. How do you know which one is Saturn?"

"You're correct," he said. "With the naked eye, it looks no different from the stars. But with a telescope . . ."

It took some time for me to correctly hold my eye to the lens. Then I saw the yellow orb that was Saturn. When Moses pointed out the rings, I was astonished.

"What are they?"

"No one knows. They may be made of thousands of tiny moons that orbit the planet so quickly and in such a thick haze, they appear to be solid. Some say they are a blur of angels, circling the planet with their ethereal wings."

One day I asked Moses, "What is a Man of the Enlightenment?"

He showed me how to hold a prism up to the sun, so that it bent the light to make a rainbow.

"A Man of the Enlightenment is someone who looks at the light and sees the rainbow," he said.

Being only four at the time, I couldn't understand what he meant. But now that I'm nine (I think) and have seen more of both light and darkness, I am certain that I, too, will one day be a Man of the Enlightenment. If only I were allowed a shard of light, I would see a world that shimmers like a glorious, heavenly rainbow.

Smothered in Darkness, I recall the many forms of light that made Versailles a paradise. The Queen's Village took up the grounds surrounding the Chateau. Maman called it her slice of Paradise and said it saved her from boredom. She used to say, "Your father is supreme ruler of France. But I am supreme ruler of Versailles." She carried a set of diamond studded silver keys to each of the buildings of her little village.

I had an open carriage all my own, painted green with yellow fleurs-de-lis. The interior, just the right size for me, was red leather. A picnic basket was mounted on a platform between the back wheels. Caesar, my kid goat, was harnessed in front, so that I may drive it through the pathways with Lisette, the Gardener's daughter, in the seat next to me.

We rode past the Grove of Domes, the Belvedere Pavilion, the Temple of Love with its statue of Cupid, the miniature opera theatre, waterfalls, moss-covered caverns, the lake with black and white swans floating among pink waterlilies, and fountains spewing water from marble statues of Greek gods.

In winter, we rode over the frozen lake in sleighs pulled by ponies, our laps covered with bear pelts.

At night, the garden was illuminated with hundreds of lights, buried in the ground so the flowers and bushes and trees and statues appeared to emit their own brilliance, while the moon reflected off decorative ponds and gushing fountains. On special occasions, Chinese fireworks were set off, bursting in the sky and reflecting off the lake in otherworldly greens, pinks, blues, reds, and purples.

Inside the palace, every room was lighted with crystal chandeliers. But the most brilliant light of all was Maman. Her face was white as marble. Her hair a luminescent silver-strawberry-blond, a unique color invented by her personal coiffure artist. Pearls glowed from strings wound into her hair, long ropes wrapped around her neck, and delicate bracelets on her wrists. Diamonds were sewn into the embroidered flowers on her satin dresses. Everything was reflected a thousand times in the Hall of Mirrors. Everywhere I looked, everything glowed and sparkled and shimmered. And at the center of it all was Maman, the sun that everyone and everything at Versailles revolved around.

I had been told my great-great-great-grandfather was the Sun King. I had no doubt that Maman was the Sun Queen. And yet, they call her the Austrian Swine.

Even after having months and months and years to think about it, I still don't understand why the French hate her so much. She told me when she first arrived from Vienna, a foreign bride of fifteen, the people loved her. But no one ever explained to me what happened to turn their adoration into murderous hatred.

Then I remember Marie told me Papa didn't have enough money to buy grain for the people to make bread, because he spent all of France's wealth helping the Americans win their Revolution. Then he tried to make more money by raising the tax on salt. But I'm not so sure he spent the *gabelle* on grain.

I do know that, when I am allowed to rule, and only have enough money to either provide my people with bread or to help someone else fight their war, I will choose bread.

Even so, I don't understand what all this had to do with Maman. She was not the King and did not command the army or set tax rates.

I rarely heard Papa and Maman being unhappy with each other, but I do remember one time. I don't know what started their conversation, but Papa blurted out, "You spend more than twice as much as any queen before you!" Then he said, "You've spent enough on your beautiful gardens to feed all of France for a year."

"What would you have me do?" Maman retorted. "Would you deprive your Queen of the only place I can find happiness? Would you deny me the refuge that is my sole comfort in this foreign land?" She began to cry. "I was forced to leave my mother at fifteen and never saw her again!"

Papa hugged her and caressed her curls. "Of course, I will do anything to make you happy, Marie."

When I have a Queen of my own, I will do everything I can to make her happy. I think about Lisette and wonder what makes her happy.

Ever since I can remember, I had played house with Lisette. Maman designed a miniature, kid-sized one-room cottage on the grounds of her mini-village, furnished with a hearth, rough-hewn table, and two little chairs. Each window held a flower box full of violets. Our play farmhouse had baby chicks running around in the yard that we could feed and a little garden of strawberries and spearmint we planted ourselves.

One morning, Lisette and I each picked a strawberry and, looking each other in the eye, popped the fruit into our mouths at the exact same moment. It tasted as sweet as if a whole bushel of strawberries had been condensed into one bite.

After that moment, I believed we were married. After all, we shared a farmhouse and had picked and eaten strawberries, grown in our own garden, at the exact same moment while looking into each other's eyes. I assumed everyone understood this.

Then one day, when Marie was complaining to Maman that she didn't want to be forced to marry at too young an age, I blurted out, *"I'm* married."

Maman's and Marie's necks snapped around to stare at me in shock, as if I had just admitted to assassinating the King of England.

"Oh, yeah?" Marie sniped, "Who's your wife?"

"Lisette."

Maman and Marie burst out laughing. I was happy, too, so I laughed with them. Though I was confused by the idea that they didn't already know about me being married to Lisette. Hadn't they seen us in our house?

Maman wiped the laugh-tears from her eyes and opened her arms. I ran into them, and she pulled me onto her lap.

"You're quite the Prince Charming," she said, tousling my hair. "Lisette is a pretty little girl."

I wonder where Lisette and her father are now. I learned from Papa's grumbling over the newspapers that Versailles has been abandoned, the gardens overgrown, and the entrance gate guarded night and day, so that we may never sneak back home.

I wonder where the peasants and servants who worked in Maman's Paradise have gone. Were they beheaded for having worked for the King and Queen? Have they been left to wander the roads around Paris like vagabonds?

Papa used to say he wished he had been born a locksmith instead of a King. I never understood this because I believed being King made him the greatest man in the world.

Now I wish I had been born to become a gardener's apprentice. I might be wandering along the road in rags, with nothing to eat but the dirt beneath my feet. But if Lisette were by my side, I would feel richer than the entire line of Bourbon Kings who came before me put together.

When Maman started getting a headache from Marie and I running around yelling and screaming and laughing, she would say, "Silence is golden."

But she was wrong. Silence is torture.

It is the Silence, even more than the Darkness, that makes me feel as if I'm losing my mind. To stay sane, I remind myself of the many wonderful sounds that filled my life in Versailles.

The music that wafted into my bedchamber as I drifted off to sleep. Maman invited the greatest musicians and composers of Europe to give chamber concerts for her closest friends. Sometimes she brought me to her private opera house, where she dressed as a shepherdess and sang songs about the simple joys of peasant life.

I miss the voice of my sister. I used to think of her as a tyrant, telling me what I could and could not do. Reminding me of all the things she could do that I could not. Making me feel stupid and calling me foolish.

Now I smile, remembering the painful sound of her harp lessons, which she hated. Oh, what I would give now, for five minutes of hearing my sister play the harp badly!

Other sounds I remember were the barking and roughhousing of dogs. Everyone in the family, including my aunts, had their own breed of dog. Greyhounds. Lapdogs. Hunting dogs. The long hallways were teaming with dogs of all sizes, their nails clicking against the marble floors, their tongues out, panting with excitement, as if each moment of their existence was the happiest of their entire lives.

I miss the tinkling of crystal goblets and clinking of silver forks against porcelain plates, as Maman and her friends dined late into the night. Most of all, I remember Maman and her friends laughing. Maman had the loveliest laugh in all of France. Her friends made a game of trying to emulate her magnificent giggle.

9

Eternal Darkness

The once-a-day meals that I used to look forward to—even though I hated them—I now dread. The food I dump on the floor is just more rotting garbage. I only hope I die of starvation before I'm buried alive in my own festering waste.

Alexander notices that I've stopped eating. He brings me a chestnut from the floor.

"Thank you, Alexander," I say. So as not to be rude, I eat the rancid nut.

Then he brings me another one. And another. Until I have eaten six and am quite full.

Alexander the Great refuses to let me starve. Which is one of the things that makes him so great.

He brings me other things, too. Objects he finds in the walls and corners of the Tower.

A silk ribbon, like my sister used to wear in her hair.

"Thank you, Alexander," I say, tying it around my wrist. "This is a great ribbon."

He makes his squeaky noise, which I'm pretty sure means, "You're welcome," but could also mean, "I have no idea what you are saying, you bizarre little boy."

He brings me a ring, set with a large gem. I try it on my fingers but it's too big, so I wear it on my thumb.

He brings me a toy soldier. In the Darkness I can't see the colors of his uniform, so I don't know if he is French, English, Austrian, or American. I decided to call him after the Marquis de Lafayette.

Next, my rat friend brings me something that feels like a pebble.

"Thank you for the rock," I say. "You shouldn't have."

For some stupid reason, I test it with my teeth. A horrific taste invades my mouth. I gag and spit. The foulness lingers on my tongue.

Rotten cheese.

"Really," I tell him. "You *shouldn't* have."

Alexander chuckles his squeaky rat chuckle. His idea of a joke.

Then he brings me what I swear is the bone of a child's finger.

I scratch the stone walls with ragged claws until my own fingers bleed.

Darkness is not a place. This is not a room in a tower.

I could be in total Darkness in a cave in Mongolia.

Or complete Darkness in a dungeon in Istanbul.

Or absolute Darkness in a black marble box, buried a hundred miles beneath the surface of the earth.

Or profound Darkness at the bottom of the ocean.

Or the eternal Darkness of deep space, millions of miles from the nearest star.

There is no Time in Darkness.
I'm always HERE.
And it's always NOW.

I am the King of Darkness.
King of Silence.
King of Nothing.
King Turd.

The Darkness is a great beast that swallowed me whole. Its noxious stomach acids corrode my skin and seep into my pores to devour my organs.

I fester. I am disintegrating into a gooey mass inside a dry husk.

I am the Ghost of the Temple Tower. I haunt the dreams of the wicked men who threw me into Darkness and left me for dead.

I have become one with the Darkness. My essence fills the cell like a noxious miasma that lingers in the cracks between the stones.

I am lucky, Alexander the Great, that you are such a good listener. I have been going on and on about Darkness. And Silence. And Time.

144

Any normal person would be sick of me by now. But you keep tickling my ear with your whiskers, whispering that I'm still a living, breathing human boy.

10

The Darkness
1 September 1794

A hinge creaks. A blade of light slices the Darkness. Alexander scurries into his nook.

"Louis?" a man's voice asks tentatively.

I lay in my wooden box. Silent. Unmoving.

The door creaks open wider. Light stabs my eyes like a talon.

"Is he alive?"

I feel as if I could answer, could make the correct sounds come out of my mouth. But a deeper part of me refuses. Even in my ethereal state, I remember that my words can be used against me.

"Louis?" the man asks, with greater urgency. "Are you alive?"

Just barely. I half hope they will think I am dead and dispose of my remains accordingly. I'm not entirely certain that I am not already dead.

Others have entered behind him. I hear deep gasps. I'm not sure if it's the noxious air or my rotting corpse that shocks them most.

"Bring me a candle," he demands.

I sense the glow. Smell the wax. Feel the warmth. I am the oldest man in the world, greeted by a priest who has come to administer Supreme Unction and issue my Last Rites.

"I am Paul Barras," the man says. "Commander of the Army of the Interior."

I have never met this man. He is my jailer. He probably voted to behead my father. Maybe my mother, too. But I feel toward him an overwhelming sense of gratitude, simply for allowing me to hear the sound of a human voice. I feel as if I could fall at his feet, hug his legs, and weep with relief.

The candle is held closer to my face.

"My God!"

Someone rushes out, retching. I try to force my eyes open, so they will see I'm not an apparition, but the relentless light seals my lids shut.

I sense the candle flame, sweeping down the length of my body. I peek out through the tiniest slit, lifting my fingertips to demonstrate that I am a sentient being.

"He's alive," President Barras announces. He continues, as if dictating an official report, "He is covered in scaly, oozing rashes. His scalp is festering with gray-green patches of fungus and crawling with lice. His skin is full of scabs and flea bites and sores and puss. He is nothing more than a sack of bones."

I am a disgusting mass of rotting flesh, crawling with vermin, decomposing in my own waste.

"Lift him," Barras orders.

"Yes, Sir," a soldier responds.

I feel like a princess in a fairy tale, rescued by a noble knight on a white horse. Except the men rescuing me are the very same men who murdered my father and mother and condemned me to Darkness.

"He must be bathed. With good soap. Find a charwoman. Make sure the water is clean. And hot."

The breeze is crisp and cool. It smells like autumn. I imagine yellow, gold, orange, and red leaves rustling on the trees. I hear them crunching underfoot, as people stroll the paths of the park that surrounds the Tower.

Children screech in play. I recall that I was once a child, frolicking in Maman's Paradise.

I wonder what year it is. If the Revolution is over. I picture myself rushed in a coach and six to Reims. Carried to the Throne. Propped up by reverent hands. Crowned amidst relieved cheers. Women weeping with joy. Chants of *"Vive le Roi!"*

"The floor is littered with rotting food and crawling with roaches," President Barras calls out from the Darkness. "Did no one notice he stopped eating?"

A few clear their throats. Reynard is not there. If he were, he would have plenty to say. I can imagine the guards shrugging with indifference, confident that this is not their responsibility. That they are not to blame.

"Damn Robespierre to Hell!" President Barras hisses.

I gather from their talk that the Incorruptible was deposed as a tyrant and sent to the guillotine. Papa made me swear never to seek vengeance against the regicides. But I do not pity Maximilien Robespierre.

Death to the Green-eyed Monster!

Little by little, I can force one eye half-open.

A charwoman arrives. A very old woman, beyond sympathy. I scream when she tries to undress me. My tattered linens have grown into my skin, fused with the scabs. My clothing must be cut off with scissors. They leave patches of cloth around the areas where it has fused with my skin.

I have a terrible thought. What if, after they inspect me for their report and bathe me, they throw me back into the Darkness? I would rather jump out the window and splatter my guts on the plaza than go back in that room. Into a grave that won't let me die.

My head is shaven to deprive the lice of the kingdom they have ruled for so long. I am bathed and dressed in fresh linens. A doctor arrives. I listen to everything everyone says about me, as I am cleaned and examined and discussed.

When I try to stand, I collapse to the floor like Punch with his strings cut. My legs are unnaturally twisted and curved.

"How old is he?" the doctor asks.

"Nine," Barras replies.

Still nine?

In Darkness, time stands still. The body ages, but the years refuse to progress.

"His bones have grown soft and deformed from lack of nutrition, sunshine, and exercise," the Doctor reports. "His knees and elbows are covered in tumors the size of a fist."

It turns out bones need sunlight to stay strong and straight.

I am put to bed with a soft, clean blanket. The closet is cleaned, the doorway bricked in and covered with concrete. I worry that Alexander has been sealed in. But he has his secret passages and will soon find me.

11

The Tower
October 1794

In Reynard's resignation letter, which is read aloud to me, he claims I am a Royal Pain in the Arse. My new guardian's name is Laurent. He is from the island of Saint Domingue.

The Government Men would very much like for me to speak. I am accused of Royal Stubbornness and addressed as the Royal Imbecile.

It is not out of stubbornness that I remain silent. The idea of speaking fills me with terror. I haven't forgotten they were determined to chop off Papa's head, no matter what pleas he made during his trial. The more he said, the more reason he gave them to find him guilty.

Laurent moves my bed beneath the window so I can kneel on the mattress, rest my elbows on the stone sill, and look out the iron bars.

I used to hate this city. The streets overflowing with regicidal mobs. The Conciergerie dungeon, where prisoners wait to be guillotined. The National Assembly Hall, where they voted to execute Papa. The *Place de la Revolution*, where Papa was beheaded. And the gates of the Tuileries, where the guillotine now stands, its blade glinting in the Autumn sun.

Papa once pointed out to me all the places in Paris built by or dedicated to Kings named Louis. The Isle San Louis, named for the patron saint of all seventeen Bourbon kings named Louis. The domed *Église Sainte-Chapelle*, built by Louis IX. Dauphin Plaza, a triangular park built by Henry IV in honor of his son and heir, who became Louis XIII, my great-great-great-great grandfather. The Hotel des Invalides, built by Louis XIV, my great-great-great-grandfather, for aged and disabled military veterans. *L'église Saint-Louis*, in the center of the hospital grounds, with its gold-plated dome that reflects the brilliance of the sun.

The Palais Royal used to belong to Papa's cousin, the duc d'Orleans, until he made it into a public park, with gardens, theatres, and walkways along an arcade of cafes and gift shops, that he gave to the people of Paris.

Marie told me the duc d'Orleans was the swing vote in favor of beheading Papa. She said it was because he hated Maman and wanted to be the next King instead of me. The people called him the Citizen King—until his son, the duc de Chartres, joined Maman's Austrian nephew, Holy Roman Emperor Frances II, in fighting against revolutionary France.

Just before I was snatched away from Maman, Marie read in a newspaper that the elder duc d'Orleans had been arrested because of his son's disloyalty to the Revolution. When I ask Laurent, he tells me the elder duke was guillotined last November.

"I understand what it's like to want to be free," Laurent says. "At your age, I was a slave, picking cane in the sugar fields."

"Did they keep you in Darkness?" I ask.

It's the first time I have said anything to anyone since I was extracted from the Darkness. I am relieved that Laurent doesn't make a big to-do about it. Or run to the Government Men so they can put it in their report.

"Yes. But not in a closet, as you were. I was forced to work under a blazing hot sun, *from cain't see to cain't see,* with no water. The heat was brutal."

"Cain't see?"

"From before sunup, when it's still so dark you can't see, to long after sundown, when it gets so dark you can't see," he explains.

"Were you all by yourself?"

"I was surrounded by hundreds of other slaves."

"Did they chop off your papa's head?"

"I never knew my parents. They were sold away before I can remember."

"How did you survive?" It was the kind of question I never would have thought to ask—before the Darkness.

"I sang."

"Revolutionary songs?" I think of the wicked songs Reynard and his friends made me sing about Maman.

"Not other peoples' songs. Songs I made up."

"What about?"

"About the heat. The sun. The sugar cane. The cuts on my hands from picking it. Songs about never knowing my mother and father. About wanting to be free."

"I think it would make me feel worse if I sang about the terrible things that have happened to me," I say.

Laurent nods thoughtfully.

"Would you tell me about something bad that happened to you, that you made a song about?"

After having no one to talk to for so long, I can't get enough of talking to Laurent.

"I used to run away. The first time I got caught, I was whipped. The second time . . ."

He pulls down his shirt collar. A deep scar the size of my hand covers the right side of his chest. The skin is indented and puckered pink and red. A design has been burned into his flesh. A three-petaled flower.

"The *fleur de lis!*"

At Versailles, everything was decorated with the three-petaled white orchid. The frames of the paintings that hung in the corridors were carved with gilt *fleurs-de-lis*. The chandeliers hung with crystal dewdrops shaped like *fleurs-de-lis*.

Golden *fleurs-de-lis* were embroidered on Maman's capes and shawls and pillow covers. The lace that hung from the sleeves and necklines of her dresses was crocheted in delicate vines of *fleurs-de-lis*. She wore a silver *fleur-de-lis* hat-pin, studded with amethysts.

In Papa's coronation portrait, he wears a bulky robe of purple velvet, lined with ermine and festooned with golden *fleurs-de-lis*. His crown sits on a cushioned stool of deep blue, embroidered with *fleurs-de-lis*. The peak of the crown is a gold *fleur-de-lis* embedded with jewels. In his military portraits, his chest is covered with bronze medals stamped with *fleurs-de-lis*. (Even though, Marie told me, he never served a single day in the military.)

The posts of the gilt iron fence that surrounded the Versailles grounds were tipped with *fleurs-de-lis* spikes.

"I was branded," Laurent says, "By the man who believed he owned me."

The cows, sheep, and goats in Maman's farm village were branded with *fleurs-de-lis*, so if they got lost, everyone would know they belonged to the Queen. I'm certain our livestock were branded with the exact same *fleur-de-lis* design as the one on Laurent's chest. As if the branding iron had been forged by the same blacksmith.

I am horrified to see that Laurent, so sweet and kind and wise, was treated no better than a beast. And with a symbol that means only one thing: the Bourbon family line. My royal blood.

"If Papa had known about this," I say, "he would have stopped it."

Laurent looks uncertain for a moment. "Your Papa was well aware of the conditions of slavery in his colonies."

"How do you know? You never even met my Papa."

"Anti-slavery delegations from San Domingue sought audiences with the King many times. They brought detailed reports of the cruelty and inhumanity of slavery."

"My Papa would have cried, if he knew what happened to you."

"I don't know about that. But he had no interest in abolishing slavery."

"Why would he allow such cruelty, in his own kingdom?"

"Have you ever eaten food that was sweetened with sugar?"

"Of course."

"Your father well knew that every granule of sugar on his table came from the blood, sweat, and tears of slaves in his Caribbean colonies. Every speck of sugar in Europe is saturated with human blood. You, yourself, Little Man, may have eaten a tart made with sugar from cane I myself picked with my own hands."

"The blood of slaves?" I ask, to be certain I understand correctly.

"The same is true of pepper, cinnamon, nutmeg, and chocolate" he adds. "Though not all from the Caribbean."

In the mornings, Maman used to spoon feed me from a cup of hot chocolate. I wonder if I could have tasted the blood of slaves, mixed with the fresh cream.

I feel as if Laurent is speaking of a man foreign to me. Not my kind, gentle, loving Papa, who spent his final days with his face in his hands.

"Papa would never allow such cruelty to his own subjects," I tell him. "He never shed a single drop of French blood."

"Slaves were not citizens, Little Man. Not while your Papa reigned."

"Does it hurt?" I ask.

"Not now. At the time, you cannot imagine the feeling of a hot iron, pressed into your skin. Held there till you can smell your own flesh searing. It took weeks to heal. I couldn't wear a shirt because I couldn't bear the touch of the fabric on my scorched skin."

When the Government Men brought me out of the Darkness and tried to remove the shirt that had grown into my sores, it felt as if my skin was being ripped off in shreds. I imagine being branded is a thousand times worse.

"As I lay there, I made up a song about running away. Being whipped. Running away again. Being branded."

"Did your song make you feel better?"

"It didn't make the wound heal faster. It didn't free me from bondage. And it didn't end slavery. But it reminded me that I'm still my own person.

No amount of whipping or branding can take my story away from me."

"I have a story."

"I know you do, Little Man."

I like it that he calls me Little Man.

I think of the wicked songs Reynard and his friends made me sing about Maman. "But I think singing it would make me feel worse."

"Your story doesn't have to be a song," Laurent explains. "Your story can be a story."

"Like a Mother Goose tale?"

"Yes," he says. "But you may not find yourself a king in a castle, married to a beautiful princess in the end."

"I know," I say. "They will never let me rule as their King."

I hadn't realized, until I say it, that this is true. It is a relief to say it aloud.

"You don't need to be King of France to be your own person. As long as you can tell your own story, you will always be your own person. Look at me. I was a slave for the first seventeen years of my life. But I've always been my own person."

"Mother Goose wrote her stories in a book so others can read them," I say. "If I wrote my story on paper, the Government Men would use it as evidence against me."

During the final days of Papa's trial, they found a secret, locked chest in his chambers, filled with personal letters. These documents were used as evidence to prove beyond the shadow of a doubt that he was a Tyrant.

"What matters is that you tell your story to *yourself*. Even if no one else will ever hear you. It's still *your* story."

Even if you tell it to a rat, I think, though I haven't seen Alexander the Great since I was released from the Darkness.

I almost tell Laurent about Alexander. How I whispered to him as I lay in the Darkness. But I'm afraid he would report to the guards about rats in my cell and they would bring arsenic to poison Alexander.

Laurent is a good man. But even good men hate rats.

12

Laurent is given permission to carry me to the battlement. The area surrounding the Tower is heavily guarded, but the rest of the Temple grounds are a public park, crisscrossed by walking paths lined with chestnut trees.

The sky is gray. The air carries a brisk chill. The branches are bare, the ground covered with a tapestry of dry leaves. A girl and a man stand just outside the perimeter of guards, looking up at the Tower.

"Does everyone know I'm here?" I ask.

"Everyone who reads the papers," Laurent says. "Though you and your sister are mentioned less and less."

The father and daughter crane their necks to see the top of the turret. I think they are smiling at me, but their faces are blurry. I can no longer see well at a distance. The physician said all those months in Darkness caused deterioration of my ocular function.

The girl waves. I'm astonished. Laurent is looking out over the Seine and doesn't notice. I lift my hand slowly, fearing a trap. Will they be accused of giving me a secret signal and guillotined for treason?

I decide to take the risk. If they *are* giving me a secret signal, I want to encourage them to plot my release, and Marie's. I wave, not high in the air but in front of my face. The girl jumps up and down, waving both hands over her head.

Could it be Lisette?

I don't want Laurent to see me waving or he would have to report it, so I stop. I smile at them, though I don't think they can see my face. A guard approaches the father and daughter. They stroll off. I look away, so as not to arouse suspicion.

Shallow patches of dirt have collected in the cracks and crevices of the ancient stones of the battlements.

"Do you think I may be given a few seeds to plant?" I ask Laurent.

"I will try, Little Man."

At Versailles, everything was flowers. In the Queen's Village there was an English garden, a Chinese garden, and a French garden. In the greenhouse, we picked and ate pineapples from the tropics, strawberries from South America, and prickly pears from the desert.

Throughout the palace, fresh cut hyacinths were arranged in large, decorative pots. Flowers were embroidered on Maman's dresses and shoes and adorned her hats. Couches, chairs, and wallpaper were decorated with thick vines. Flowers were carved into the woodwork of chairs, tables, and desks. We ate from plates edged with rings of intertwined violets and pearls, designed by the Royal porcelain factory. A special type of hyacinth was named *Maria Antonia* because it was Mamon's favorite.

A week later, Laurent brings me a leather pouch of brown seeds.

"What are they?"

"Let's plant them and find out."

We take the seeds to the top of the Tower. I gaze down at the park from every angle, but Lisette and her father are not there. I press each one into the shallow soil. Every day, Laurent checks on them for me.

A couple weeks later, he carries me to the battlement, where one flower has blossomed, deep purple with velvety petals. The rest have died in the dirt. Seeing the lonely violet, I burst into tears.

"What makes you so sad, Little Man?"

"Maman is dead, isn't she?"

"Yes," he says softly.

When I was eight, I could only survive by believing Maman was in the cell above me, whispering through the stones. But now that I'm nine, the truth is a relief.

"Will you let me see her cell?"

"If it's unlocked."

On our way down, we stop at the door to the room where I last saw Maman and Marie. The only information I've gotten about Marie for more than a year is that she was transferred to a different tower the same day Maman was transferred to the Conciergerie Prison. Laurent has warned me anyone caught passing notes or other communication between us will be deemed treasonous.

Laurent turns the knob easily and opens it. The room looks exactly as I remembered it. I didn't think about it at the time, but I now realize that, when the three of us were there together, Maman gave Marie and me the bed, while she slept on the stone floor.

"Maman is dead," I whisper.

That night I tell Laurent, "I think I should like to be a gardener. I would plant so many seeds that no flower would ever have to grow alone."

"You would make a brilliant gardener," he assures me.

"Why is that?"

"Because you have a big heart."

I remember something Marie told me when I was seven that I didn't understand at the time.

174

"Why does everyone hate Maman and Papa?" I had asked.

"When the Americans had their Revolution against King George, Papa sent thousands of French troops and ammunition and ships to help them."

"Because England is our enemy and we hate King George," I added. In my playroom at Versailles, I had whole regiments of French, American, and English soldiers. The English were always the enemy, and the French always helped the Americans to defeat them.

"When the Americans won their Revolution, Papa discovered he had spent all of our government's money helping them. France was nearly bankrupt. Then France had a year of crop failures. And another. And another. Half of France didn't have enough grain for bread. If Papa hadn't spent all our money helping the Americans, he could have bought grain from other countries, enough to feed all of France. But there was no money. Hundreds of thousands of French starved to death."

"But we helped the Americans to beat the English. We humiliated King George."

"What did that gain for the French?" Marie asked.

"We can hold our heads high, knowing we are better than the English."

"You can't exactly hold your head high if you're starving," Marie said. "On top of that, Papa kept raising the tax on salt, to make up for the deficit. Now the people had even less money to spend on what little bread was available. And because it was scarce, the price of bread was astronomical. The whole time, through years of famine, Maman was spending the nation's money on priceless jewels and lavish parties for her friends."

Laurent says solemnly, "While your family and their friends were feasting on veal, venison, fine cheeses, Belgian pastries, and

Portuguese wine, hundreds of thousands of children starved to death, all over France."

"If I had known, I would have shared my food with the starving children."

"As to why your Papa and Maman ignored the suffering of their people, I do not know."

This makes me think of a question I once asked Maman, during Papa's trial.

"Why does Papa put his face in his hands?" I asked.

"Because," she said, "he doesn't know what to do."

"About what?"

"About France. About the Revolution. About us."

"But he's the King. It's his job to know what is best for France," I insisted.

"When your Papa was fourteen, *his* father— your grandfather—who was supposed to be the next King, died of the King's Evil. Your father's mother and brother, who was the original

Dauphin, had already died of the same disease. Your father was only eighteen when *his* grandfather died and he became King Louis XVI," she explained. "He knew nothing about how to run a country, so he let his advisors make all the decisions. Instead of learning from them, he preferred to go hunting. Now, when there is no one left to advise him, he feels helpless."

"You can advise him," I suggested.

"I've told him we must allow our foreign allies to go to war against the Revolutionaries. To defeat them and restore him to the throne. But he refuses to make war on the French people."

Then I asked a question I had been wondering for a long time. "Why doesn't Papa wear a crown and sit on a throne, like the kings in fairy tales?"

Maman laughed. "Thrones and crowns are old fashioned. The only time your father ever sat on a throne and wore a crown was the day of his Coronation. Even then, he complained that it was uncomfortable."

That night as I lay on my bed in the Tower, I wonder why Maman and Papa didn't have big enough hearts to feed the children of France.

Or free the slaves.

13

The Tower
Christmas 1794

Laurent tells me I'm going to have important visitors on Christmas Day. I know by now that "visitors" are Government Men. And they are coming to inspect me.

The charwoman brings me a sailor suit. I'm surprised that it's new and fits comfortably. Normally, I wear only a sleeping shirt and under-linens, with no breaches or shoes.

"I had a little boy like you, once," the charwoman says, regarding me with a brittle aspect. "A grandson."

I do not respond. I suspect she is one of the angry women who cheered as Maman's severed head was held up for all to see.

"He starved to death," she adds. "The same day the Austrian Bitch was seen at the opera in her Smallpox Coiffure."

The smallpox inoculation was a new medical treatment that many people were afraid of, but Maman was a believer in scientific medicine and wanted everyone to know it was a good thing. After the first Dauphin, Marie, and I were inoculated, she asked Leonard to create a hairdo and hat combination in celebration of the treatment. I was barely four at the time, and don't remember being inoculated, but I do remember Maman's *coiffure*.

I used to love visiting Leonard's workshop, a little building on the Versailles grounds where his creations sat proudly on marble pedestals, like busts of composers in the music room. My favorite was a pirate ship hat with black, skull-and-crossbones sails, floating in waves of blue foam-frosted hair.

Leonard began Maman's smallpox coiffure with a wire scaffolding that he erected on the crown of her head. He stood on a stool to wind her hair around the cylinder until it stood a foot high, then added a hat that was decorated with an olive tree made from twisted silver wire. The leaves were green silk embroidered with gold thread and the olives were emeralds. He coiled a black ruby-eyed snake around the base of the tree and wound a garland up the trunk.

"The tree and fruit represent the force of life," he explained, "The serpent is the deadly disease. The garland is the life-saving vaccine."

Had Maman been in her box at the Opera House, showing off her smallpox coiffure, while the charwoman's grandson was laying on a pallet in a dark room, taking his last hungry breath?

Laurent warned me the Government Men like to report that they found me, "playing quietly." I sit on the floor, playing *vent-et-un* with myself, while they scrutinize me and make their official comments.

I deal out my first card from a Revolutionary deck Laurent won from another soldier in a game of dice. A Joker.

"How are you, Little Capet?" the first Government Man asks.

I deal out my second card. Lady Liberty, who used to be the Queen. Twenty-one. I win.

"The Royal Foetus refuses to speak," the second Government Man says. "He is the filthy scion of a corrupt bloodline."

I start a new round, as if I haven't heard. My first card is a Voltaire, the philosopher whose profile replaced the King. The second is Rousseau, who replaced the Jack.

"Make him stand up," the third Government Man demands.

I am as weak as an infant. I cannot get up or stand on my own. Laurent helps me to ease up to a standing position and sits me on the edge of the bed. I can sit up more or less straight by holding my arms out to my sides, like the flying buttresses that prop up the outer walls of Notre Dame Cathedral.

"Even in this state of decrepitude," the second man comments, "he is a rallying point for the Royalists."

"Is there anything you need?" the first man asks.

I can barely hide a smirk. Every time the Government Men come to observe me and make their reports, they ask, "Is there anything you need?"

I want to say, "Could you be so kind as to dig up the heads of my Maman and Papa, sew them back onto their bodies, and revive them to life?"

Laurent often tells me that suffering so unfairly has made me bitter. I have a flash of insight about the charwomen. What kind of Darkness has she suffered, to make her so bitter?

"Wouldn't you like a Christmas sweet?" the first man asks, holding out a candy wrapped in gold foil.

I pretend not to understand the offer. I fear it is meant to poison me.

At Versailles, Papa used to have a Royal Taster whose job was to take a sip of everything in his cup and a bite of everything on his plate, before Papa himself ate and drank it. When I was little, I thought the Royal Taster's job was to make sure everything tasted delicious. Then my sister told me his job was to test Papa's food for poison.

The Royal Taster had a lilting accent, like Laurent's. I realize now that he must have been a slave. No sane, free person would choose to test food and drink for poison. Not for all the diamonds in Maman's hair. Each morsel from Papa's plate and every drop of wine from his goblet that touched the Royal Taster's lips must have filled him with terror.

The Government Men order the charwoman to bring fresh grapes. I am handed a small bunch of dark purple fruit. These I accept, confident they cannot be injected with poison, or I would have noticed tiny holes in the skin.

I want to save them to share with Alexander, but the Government Men are determined to observe as I eat. I pluck one grape, place it in my mouth and roll it around. The skin is smooth on my tongue. I suck on it to release the juice, gumming rather than chewing.

Before I was imprisoned, I had been losing baby teeth and was excited to soon get my big boy teeth. In the Darkness, more baby teeth fell out, but no big teeth grew in to replace them. The physician said being deficient in calcium, my body had nothing to generate new teeth with.

Maman used to read to me about the ancient Greek gods, who ate manna and drank ambrosia. "Food and drink that tastes so good, it cannot be described. Fit only for the gods." On Christmas Day, 1794, I am convinced fresh grapes are manna and their juice is ambrosia.

I eat so slowly, the Government Men become bored and take their leave.

I save three grapes for Alexander. He deserves to eat manna and drink ambrosia as much as any god. I haven't seen him since the

Darkness, but I know he will visit me as soon as he feels it's safe.

14

The Tower
Winter 1795

You and your sister are being debated by the National Convention," Laurent tells me.

He's reading *Ami du Peuple*.

"What are they saying about us?"

"Discussing whether you should remain imprisoned or be sent into exile."

Exile is not a place I would have wanted to go in the old days, but now, anywhere sounds better than Paris, France.

"Please read more," I beg.

"'Capet'—" Laurent looks up. "That's you."

"They should not call me that. I am King Louis XVII."

"Don't ever say that!" Laurent growls, grabbing my collar. "We could both be thrown from the battlements for those words."

I know I shouldn't have said it. I know the people of France do not want me to rule as their King, even though it is my right.

"Promise you will never say that again," Laurent cautions. "Or I will request that I be transferred to a different post."

"I promise."

I understand by now that words are a matter of life and death. My life depends on words the Government Men use to describe me in their reports. Words I call myself in front of others. Words used by angry mobs to express their hatred for Maman.

The words "Yes" or "No," which the Assembly men uttered, when voting whether or not to behead King Louis XVI. Papa was executed based on a difference of one vote. If just one man had uttered the word "No" instead of "Yes," my Maman and Papa would still be alive.

Laurent continues reading. "Minister Cambacérès, of the Committee of Public Safety, argued that, 'The exile of a tyrant has always been the first step in his return to power.'"

"How can I return to power if I was never in power in the first place?" I ask.

Laurent presses his lips together and says nothing.

One morning, when Laurent tries to help me out of bed, I scream in agony. Every movement of my limbs is so painful, he can't even prop me against the wall to sit. He tells the guard to summon a doctor. A Government Man arrives.

"There are many children far sicker than you, Royal Capet," he tells me. "All over France, children whose lives are worth more than yours are starving to death for want of bread. You don't deserve to see a doctor."

When he leaves, I ask Laurent, "What does he mean that children all over France starve to death every day?"

"There's been a series of bad harvests. There isn't enough grain to make bread for everyone. What little bread there is, is absurdly expensive."

"It's been two years since they executed Papa," I say. "How are the children still starving? Didn't murdering my Maman and Papa solve their problems?"

Laurent shakes his head. "The Revolution is five years old. And still, men, women, and children continue to starve."

"Then, what was it all for?" I ask. "Has any good come of the Revolution?"

"Last year, the National Convention voted to free all slaves in French colonies."

"What did you do when you learned you were free?"

"All I wanted was to go to Paris. But I had no money to travel. I continued to pick cane on my former Master's plantation. But now he could no longer whip or brand me. And he had to pay me. I worked long enough to buy passage to France. I arrived in Nantes in September and walked to Paris on foot. I signed up for the National Guard and was commissioned to serve as caretaker for the deposed King and Queen's orphaned son."

"I'm glad it's you," I say.

I can no longer get out of bed. The slightest movement is agony. Some days, if I'm feeling well enough, Laurent holds me up to the window to gaze out for a few moments.

I have not seen Lisette and her father for weeks. Not since the day we waved at each other from the battlement.

"I've brought you a physician. A secret Royalist," Laurent whispers. It is the middle of the night.

The doctor gently lifts my arm, bends my elbow. I whimper with pain. He rotates my wrist, then repeats the same exam on my other arm and both legs.

"The King's Evil," he concludes. "The same disease his grandfather and uncle had."

"My brother, the first Dauphin, died of the King's Evil," I tell him.

The doctor prescribes a tisane of herbs and spices, mixed with sugar and rum, warmed over the fire. When he's gone, I ask Laurent, "Does the sugar have blood in it? From the suffering of slaves?"

"It's okay to drink it," he says.

The doctor's brew is soothing and makes me sleepy.

"I think a government cannot be truly good if it ignores the suffering of children," I mumble.

I'm not sure if I actually say it, or only think it.

15

The Tower
Spring 1795

I am awoken by a strange man. A soldier.

"What have they done to Laurent?" I ask.

My first thought is that he was guillotined as a traitor, for being too kind to me. Or for calling in the Royalist doctor. In my panic, I try to sit up, but cannot.

"He set sail for the Caribbean this morning. I'm Etienne."

"Has he been captured back into slavery?"

"He's sailing to San Domingue to be married to his childhood sweetheart. He lost track of her after they were freed, but he recently relocated her and signed up with a regiment that shipped out this morning. He wanted me to tell you he's sorry he didn't have time to say goodbye."

"How do I know you're telling the truth?" I ask.

Since when do I trust anything a Government Man tells me?

"We were in the same regiment." Etienne removes a slip of paper from his jacket and hands it to me. "He asked me to give you this."

I can just barely make out Laurent's strange script. It says:

Tell your story. Be your own man.

Etienne has a habit of crumpling up his newspaper and shoving it under my bed after he reads it. I rifle through the pages, looking for information about my family.

I learn that more than 2,000 French citizens were guillotined over a period of two years. I learn that Leonard, Maman's hat and wig designer, was guillotined. My Aunt Elisabeth was guillotined. Maman's best friend, Princess Lambelle, was beheaded by a mob, her head paraded through the streets on a pike.

Robespierre, the Green-Eyed-Monster, with his endless lists of Enemies of the State, was declared an Enemy of the State and guillotined before a cheering crowd of thousands.

I learn that, after all the beheadings, 3,000 homeless dogs, their owners executed, roamed the streets of Paris. Because they were deemed a threat to public health and safety, the National Guard was sent out to shoot them one night. The next morning, hundreds of wagons carted the dog carcasses to a mass grave outside the city.

When I run out of current papers, I rifle through a bin of old papers by the hearth, used for kindling. I come across a headline printed two-and-a-half years ago.

Deposed Queen Appeals to all Mothers

In the early morning hours of 16 October 1793, Marie Antoinette was carted by tumbril from the Conciergerie to the gates of the Tuileries. Onlookers threw rotten food and worse and taunted her with names that cannot be put into print.

At the scaffolding, the Queen was stripped to her chemise. She remained calm and did as she was told. At one point, she seemed to grow faint and lose her balance. She was heard to apologize with quiet dignity for stepping on the foot of the executioner.

A statement, signed by the eight-year-old Royal Capet, having witnessed all manner of crimes against France, committed by the Queen, sealed her fate. President Robespierre ruled that Marie Antoinette was "the scourge and bloodsucker of France" and sentenced her to beheading by guillotine for high treason. A sentence that surprised no one.

"I appeal to all mothers here today," the Queen pled to the crowd. "Is it right to take a mother from her dear child, who is innocent of all wrongdoing?"

The crowd, heretofore out for the Queen's blood, stood silent for the barest fraction of a second. A few, but not many, women's voices called out, "Let the Queen live!" Their plaintive calls for clemency were drowned out by thousands shouting, "Death to the Queen!"

The public has made up its mind. They are hungry for royal blood.

Will the Wolf Cub be next?

I know now that I will never be released from the Tower. It is only a question of whether I grow old in captivity or die young in captivity.

On my tenth birthday, Etienne plays the fiddle and dances a goofy jig, trying to cheer me up.

I beg him to take me to the battlement. He has strict orders never to allow me out of my cell, so he waits until the cathedral bells strike midnight to carry me up. Seeing my lonely violet, all by itself in the shallow dirt, makes me terribly sad.

As Etienne is laying me back in bed, I hear a faint rustling between my pillow and the wall.

After he leaves and I am certain the night guard has had his wine and fallen asleep on his pallet, I greet my old friend. Alexander lays on his side, tucked into the open end of the pillowcase.

"You showed up for my birthday," I whisper. I pet his belly. "You have gotten quite plump. What goodies have you been scavenging?"

His breathing is low and soft. I pet him until I fall asleep.

I awaken to faint, high-pitched squeaking.
Alexander lays on his side, surrounded by six
tiny Alexanders, nursing at his—*her*—belly.

"Alexander! You had babies."

The guard rustles on his pallet and
groans.

"I guess you're not a boy, after all," I
whisper. It wasn't as if I gave my rat friend an
anatomical inspection when we first met in
Darkness. "I'd better start calling you Alex."

Each *ratlette* is no bigger than my pinky
finger. They are hairless. Their skin is rosy
pink. Their eyes are sealed shut. Their black
eyelids look like the mask Maman used to
wear to costume balls. Their itsy-bitsy toes are
as pink as rose petals.

They nurse until they are bloated, then
crawl over and under each other until they fall

206

asleep in a pile. Alex licks them clean, her eyes half closed. She looks exhausted and contented at the same time.

Then I think of something.

"I have a gift for you," I whisper.

I pull the locket from beneath my shirt. I guess Maman's curse on anyone who tries to take it from me must have circulated through the ranks of soldiers, guards, and Government Men. There's no way they have allowed me to keep it all this time out of the goodness of their hearts.

I press the silver tab with my thumb. The locket pops open. A hint of gardenia wafts out of the chamber. The curly lock of hair is more silver than I remember it. I pick it up between my thumb and forefinger. Beneath it is another lock of hair. Darker. Shorter. Papa's. Beneath that, a few strands of fine, pale hair. My brother's.

I twist all three together and wrap them in a semi-circle around the sleeping *ratlettes*. Alex adjusts the hair with her nose, arranging it snugly around her babies to form a nest.

She looks me in the eye and squeaks, *Thank you.*

The *ratlettes'* eyes are open. Their fur shines like silver silk in the moonlight. They are strong enough to stumble around and get in little paw fights over who gets the best spot to nurse.

Alex stands and stretches. The *ratlettes* tumble over each other and squeak in protest. She grabs one in her mouth, climbs down a leg of the bed, and scurries along the wall, disappearing into a corner. A moment later, her head pokes out of a hidden chink, minus one *ratlette.*

One by one, Alex moves her babies from my bed to her new nook. Her family is ready to practice crawling through the walls of the castle, scavenging fossilized cheese leftover from some crusading knight of the Dark Ages, and finding their own hidden crannies to occupy.

She returns one last time to gather Maman's, Papa's, and Louis-Joseph's hair and move it to her new nest.

I am happy for Alex. And relieved that she and her *ratlettes* have found a safe home, but I suddenly feel incredibly lonely. Papa is dead and will never return. Maman is gone. Aunt Elizabeth is gone.

Marie is in another cell in another tower, but I hardly think of her anymore. It's easier than imagining her so close, knowing I may never see her again.

I raise myself onto my knees to gaze out the barred window. The balmy breeze caresses my cheek, like Maman's fingertips. The major streets and bridges are lined with lights.

Paris at ground level is famous for its stench, but up here, above the human waste, the air carries scents of the countryside, of freshly plowed fields that remind me of Versailles.

Someone in the park lights a candle. The flame moves slowly, flickering in and out through the newly budding branches, and emerges into a clearing below the Tower. A dear, sweet face is illuminated by the amber glow.

Lisette!

She smiles up at my window. My cell is so dark, she can't possibly see me. I would like to push my head through the bars, to grin back at her. But I can only stick my arms out up to my elbows and flail them around in a crazy double-wave.

Lisette hands the candle to her father, raises both arms above her head, jumps up and down, and mimes clapping.

I want to jump up and down on my bed with joy. But I cannot stand on my own two legs, much less jump. And I can't risk awakening the guard.

Then I think of something. I hold my index finger straight up, to signal, "Just a moment."

I pull my arms back in and remove the locket from around my neck. I grab a wad of my hair, which has grown quite long, and tug. It won't pull out. I grab a smaller clump of strands and yank hard. I can hear it rip out of my scalp as I feel the skin torn away. I tie the strand in a knot, curl it around my finger, and place it in the locket.

I stick one arm out through the bars, dangling the locket from its ribbon. I swing the locket to fling it as far out as I can. Lisette runs forward to catch it. She smiles up at me, holding the locket to her heart with both hands. I clasp my hands together through the bars, to signal our unbreakable bond.

A night watchman approaches. The candle goes out. Lisette disappears.

I feel truly happy for the first time since before they dragged me away from Maman. Before they made us move to the Tower. Before we rode from Versailles to Paris in the pouring rain. Before the angry lady yanked Maman's hair and screamed in her face.

Before our Failed Flight to Varennes, when I hid on the floor of the carriage, concealed in darkness, and the angry man demanded to know where I was. And I jumped up and said, "I'm here!"

All those terrible things happened to me. And yet, here I am. My own person. As long as I can still say, "I'm here," I'm doing okay.

My smile widens into a grin. The big, toothy kind.

I'm here!

Afterword

King Louis XVII died on 8 June 1795, ten weeks after his tenth birthday, from *scrofula* (tuberculosis of the bones and lymph glands), known at the time as the King's Evil. His death was attended by Dr. Phillippe-Jean Pelletan, who secretly removed Louis's heart and kept it preserved in a jar of formaldehyde. The rest of his remains were dumped into an unmarked grave in the cemetery of the church of Sainte-Marguerite.

In 1975, Louis's heart, preserved in secret for one hundred and eighty years, was put in a crystal urn and placed in the royal crypt of the Basilique Saint-Denis in Paris.

For over two hundred years, theories abounded that the little King had been smuggled out to safety, his death faked, and his remains those of another boy. But in the year 2000, DNA testing of the preserved heart determined conclusively that he was indeed the son of Louis XVI and Marie Antoinette.

Marie-Therese, sister of Louis XVII, was released from the Temple Tower in December 1795, around the time of her seventeenth birthday. She was taken to Vienna, where she married her cousin Louis-Antoine de Bourbon, duc d'Angouleme.

About the Author

Lizzi Wolf was born in Detroit, Michigan. She holds a B.A. from Oberlin College and a Ph.D. in American Culture from University of Michigan. Lizzi has taught college courses in Film Studies, Popular Culture, and Children's Literature at colleges in Michigan, South Carolina, and Massachusetts.

Thank you for reading *Citizen Louis-Charles*. As an independent publisher, I rely on word-of-mouth and reader recommendations to promote my novel. If you enjoyed this book, I invite you to post a rating and (if you have time) write a brief review on Amazon. LW

Acknowledgments

My sources include: *A Day with Marie Antoinette* by Hélène Delalex; *Memoirs of the Court of Marie Antoinette, Queen of France, by Madam Campan, First Lady in Waiting to the Queen*; and *The Bourbon Kings of France* by Desmond Seward.

For full-color images of Versailles and the clothes, jewelry, etc.. of Marie-Antoinette, as well as furnishing and interior décor of the chateau, the coffee-table book *Marie-Antoinette* by Hélène Delalex, Alexandre Maral, and Nicolas Milovanovic. To learn about the process of identifying Louis's heart DNA, *The Lost King of France: How DNA Solved the Mystery of the Murdered Son of Louis XVI and Marie Antoinette,* by Deborah Cadbury.

My characterization of Robespierre is partly based on *Fatal Purity: Robespierre and the French Revolution* by Ruth Scurr. An excellent discussion of the role of grain and bread shortages in the French Revolution can be found in the chapter titled, "Bread in the Nineteenth Century," in H.E. Jacob's *Six Thousand Years of Bread: Its Holy and Unholy History.*

For research on the psychological impact of solitary confinement and long-term isolation: *Hell is a Very Lonely Place: Voices from Solitary Confinement,* edited by Jean Casella, James Ridgeway, and Sarah Shourd; *Solitary Confinement: Social Death and its Afterlives* by Lisa Guenther; and *Solitary: The Inside Story of Supermax Isolation and How We Can Abolish It,* by Terry Allen Kupers. To support the rights of victims and survivors of solitary confinement, check out Solitary Watch at solitarywatch.org.

Athena's Shield

a novel of the
Spartacus Slave Revolt

"As meticulously detailed, accurate, and
colorful as a Roman wall painting."
Richard P. Martin
Professor of Classics, Stanford University

Lizzi Wolf

Lizzi Wolf

The
Versailles
of
Sadness
a novel

That's my story and I'm stickin' to it!

MEDUSA BOOKS

(8/10/2022)

Printed in Great Britain
by Amazon

12949966R00132